Seeds of Doubt

Mysteries of Sparrow Island™

SEEDS OF DOUBT

Kristin Eckhardt

Guideposts Books
CARMEL, NEW YORK

www.guideposts.org
(800) 431-2344
Guideposts Books & Inspirational Media Division

Cover and interior design by Cindy LaBreacht
Cover art by Gail W. Guth
Map by Jim Haynes, represented by Creative Freelancers, Inc.
Typeset by Nancy Tardi
Printed in the United States of America

For my wonderful grandfather, H. Lloyd Heim,
who lives his faith and loves his family.

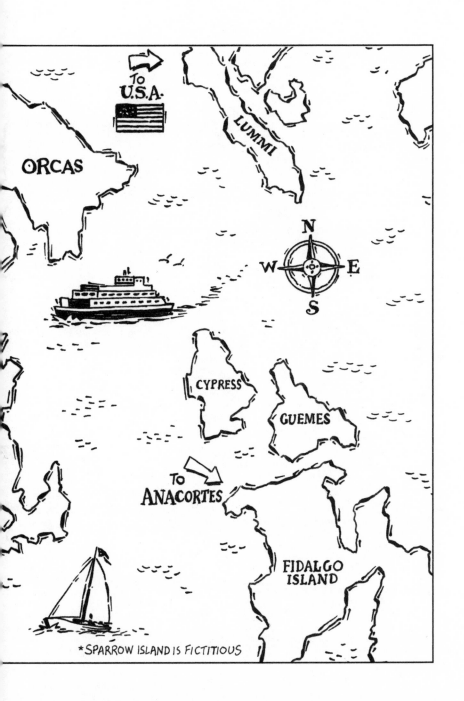

TO U.S.A.

LUMMI

ORCAS

N
W   E
S

CYPRESS

GUEMES

TO ANACORTES

FIDALGO ISLAND

*SPARROW ISLAND IS FICTITIOUS

CHAPTER ✾ ONE

Are you ready for the surprise?" Hugo Baron asked the guests seated around his dining room table.

Abby Stanton smiled up at her boss. Hugo was the Curator of the Sparrow Island Nature Conservatory and had told her to expect something unusual at his dinner party tonight. She'd been looking forward to it all week, thrilled when Saturday had finally arrived.

It was a small, cozy gathering with only Abby and her parents in attendance. Her sister Mary and her boyfriend Deputy Sheriff Henry Cobb had been invited, too, but they'd already made other plans for the evening.

Hugo had cooked a wonderful meal using recipes he'd collected from around the world. He'd traveled to many exotic places before settling on Sparrow Island twenty-six years ago.

His small timber-frame cottage was nestled in a grove of old madrone trees. As an ornithologist, Abby knew that several different birds used the trees as nesting sites and fed on their orange autumn berries. Hugo often talked about watching deer eat the creamy blossoms off the trees in the spring.

His home looked so natural there that no one would ever guess the amount of time Hugo spent to make his property as non-intrusive as possible to the native flora and fauna. He took special care not to use noxious chemicals on his small yard or to introduce any nonnative plants. Abby knew he was a strong advocate for natural habitats and had often fought against developments that would adversely affect the environment.

Abby shared his love of wildlife and the environment. She'd found a kindred spirit when he'd convinced her to become the Associate Curator at the Sparrow Island Nature Conservatory.

"I'm not sure anything can top that delicious dinner," Ellen Stanton said. "I never realized you were such an excellent cook."

The setting sun cast a golden glow through the window, bathing Abby's parents in its warm light. They were good friends with Hugo and enjoyed hearing about all his travel adventures.

"Thank you," Hugo said modestly. He stood at the head of the table, looking as distinguished as ever in a pair of neatly pressed khaki slacks and a white dress shirt. "That's quite a compliment coming from you."

Ellen's talents in the kitchen were exceeded only by her kindness and the strength of her faith. Both George and Ellen had raised Abby and her older sister Mary with that same deep faith and abiding trust in God to guide their lives.

God's divine guidance had led Abby back home again to Sparrow Island after she'd spent more than thirty-five years in New York teaching ornithology at Cornell University. Always a teacher at heart, Abby still got to share her extensive knowledge about birds and other wildlife with the many visitors who came to the beautiful San Juan Islands throughout the year.

"Do you need a drum roll?" George offered with a teasing smile.

Hugo's blue eyes lit with amusement as he nodded his assent. "If you please, sir."

George tapped his fingers on the edge of the table, simulating the rat-a-tat-tat of drumsticks.

Hugo lifted the lid off the oblong silver platter with a flourish, revealing four dessert plates.

Abby and her parents leaned forward for a closer look.

"Well?" Hugo said, waiting for their response.

"What is it?" George asked.

Hugo smiled at their quizzical expressions. "It's called Peking Dust and it was one of my favorite desserts when I visited China."

The dessert was aptly named in Abby's opinion. It resembled a mound of fine sawdust topped with a dollop of whipped cream.

"Trust me," Hugo told them as he passed out the dessert plates. "It's delicious."

Abby picked up her fork, always willing to try a new culinary adventure. Besides, she trusted Hugo. If he said it was delicious, she couldn't wait to experience it for herself.

She wasn't disappointed. The sweet delicacy melted in her mouth. "It's wonderful!"

"I've never tasted anything like it," Ellen exclaimed. "I hope you'll share the recipe."

"I'll be happy to do so." Hugo sat down at the table. "I'll never forget the first time I had this dessert." A reminiscent gleam danced in his blue eyes. "Believe it or not, I even know the date. I looked it up in my journal yesterday to find the recipe. Clarissa and I were visiting friends in the northern province of China. They were missionaries there and ran a hospital. They provided medical services and training for the Chinese women to become nurses."

Abby enjoyed hearing stories about Hugo's travels. She knew his late wife Clarissa had died from malaria while they were in Africa in the mid-seventies. Hugo still spoke of her with affection and Abby believed his faith had helped him carry on without her.

"Have you ever thought about writing an autobiography or a travel memoir?" George asked him. "You have so many fascinating stories."

Hugo chuckled at the suggestion. "I'm afraid people wouldn't believe half of them. It's amazing how the truth really is stranger than fiction."

Abby agreed. She never could have imagined returning to Sparrow Island again. Her sister's car accident had brought her back home and changed both of their lives forever.

Accepting God's plan for her life had taken some adjustment. So had living with her sister again. The accident had left Mary in a wheelchair and she'd faced some major adjustments in her life as well. They'd both had to learn how to make room for each other in their busy lives, but the two sisters had never been closer. For that, Abby was thankful every day.

Ellen took another bite of her dessert, then wrinkled her brow. "It has an unusual flavor that I can't quite place."

"Chestnuts," Hugo informed her. ""They're ground into a fine powder, then incorporated with the rest of the ingredients. That's why the dessert is called Peking Dust."

"Mary loves chestnuts," George said, speaking of his eldest daughter. "Too bad she's not here to enjoy it."

"She loves music too," Ellen reminded him. "That's why Henry surprised her with those tickets to see *Seven Brides for*

Seven Brothers in Seattle tonight. Otherwise, I know she wouldn't have missed this dinner party for anything."

Abby had witnessed Mary's turmoil over the decision herself. Hugo's dinner invitation had arrived the very same day that Henry had presented her with the tickets to the musical. Certain that her boss wouldn't be offended, Abby had encouraged her sister to go to Seattle to see the show.

"I don't blame her a bit for wanting to see the show," Hugo said. "Especially since those tickets were nonrefundable. When Mary called with her regrets I promised to have both of them over for dinner soon. In the meantime, Abby can take home some Peking Dust for them to enjoy later."

Gracious as always, Hugo had a habit of making people feel at ease no matter what the circumstances. In some ways it surprised Abby that he'd never married again. Hugo was certainly kind and handsome enough to charm any woman.

The thought made her blush, and she turned her attention back to her dessert.

"Mary's always loved music," Ellen said wistfully. "When she was a little girl she used to sing all the time. Sometimes she'd even make up her own songs."

"She does have a beautiful voice," Abby agreed, thinking about the times she'd come upon Mary unaware and heard her singing a hymn.

"I just wish she'd use that voice of hers more often," George said. "I can't remember the last time I heard her sing without the rest of the church choir drowning her out."

"Spoken like a devoted father," Abby quipped, causing the others at the table to laugh as well.

"Well, maybe so," George admitted with a wry chuckle. "I guess I'm proud of both my girls."

At fifty-five, Abby could hardly call herself a girl anymore, although she wasn't about to complain. She and Mary had been blessed with parents who had always loved and encouraged them. Mary's accident had reminded all of them to thank God for their blessings every day.

Hugo rose to his feet. "Shall we take our coffee into the living room? It's the perfect spot to view the sunset."

They followed him there and Abby found herself fascinated once more by all the unusual artifacts in Hugo's home. The décor reflected the many cultures and lands that Hugo had visited. The teak and bamboo coffee table had come from Bali. A Turkish rug adorned the hardwood floor. Boruca masks from Costa Rica accented the wall on each side of the large bay window.

Through the window, Abby could see a cedar waxwing preening itself among the leathery green leaves of a madrone tree. She smiled to herself, feeling contentment wash over her. At this moment, she couldn't think of anywhere else she'd rather be.

Hugo cleared his throat, drawing Abby's attention away from the window.

"I invited you all to dinner tonight because this is a special occasion for me," Hugo announced. "Twenty-six years ago, I set foot on Sparrow Island for the first time. I wanted to celebrate that anniversary with my good friends."

Abby took a chair next to the fireplace. The weather was cool for March, making her relish the crackling fire in the hearth. "Twenty-six years ago today?"

"That's right," Hugo affirmed. "My first trip to the San Juan Islands."

Ellen smiled up at him. "I remember the first time we met you."

"So do I," Hugo replied. He walked over to his bookcase. "In fact, I memorialized it in my journal."

He searched among the row of red, leather-bound journals, his finger running over the dates embossed in gold on the spines. Then Hugo pulled one slim red volume from the shelf.

Abby watched him leaf through it until he found the page he sought.

"Here it is." Hugo paused a moment, then began reading aloud in his rich, deep voice.

I attended the Little Flock Church on Sparrow Island this morning and was warmly welcomed by the congregation. After the service, I met a couple by the name of George and Ellen Stanton who invited me to their home for Sunday dinner. I can't remember the last time I had such a delicious meal and such stimulating conversation.

"It may have been twenty-six years ago," George interjected with a wide smile, "but I still remember that you had two slices of my wife's apple pie that day."

"How could I resist with that wonderful cinnamon ice cream on top?" Hugo asked him.

"That's my favorite too," Abby said. "Do you remember our first birding tour?"

"I certainly do," Hugo replied. "We conducted a search for the elusive marbled murrelet. That's when I knew I had to hire you to work at the conservatory. But I'm getting ahead of myself."

He turned a page in the journal, then continued reading.

I wish there was a place here to learn more about all the wildlife on the San Juan Islands. Something like the Lewa Conservatory in Kenya or the Warrawong Sanctuary in

Australia. It would be a large project to undertake, but I find the idea of it very intriguing.

"And thus the seed for the Sparrow Island Nature Conservatory was planted," George mused.

Hugo nodded. "Indeed, it was, my friend."

"No more interruptions," Ellen implored. "I want to hear the rest of the journal entry."

Hugo turned another page, his voice softer now as he finished reading the passage.

I took a walk under the stars tonight. I've never felt as close to God as I do in this place. Ever since Clarissa died I've been looking for a place to call home. I think I may have finally found it.

Abby's throat tightened at his words and she could see a sheen of tears in her mother's blue eyes.

"That's beautiful," Abby said. "It must be wonderful to have so many memories recorded over the years."

"It is." Especially when I come across a story that I've completely forgotten. We always believe that we'll remember the special moments and the special people we meet in our lives, but time has a way of making those impressions fade away."

Abby nodded. "I met hundreds of students while I was teaching at Cornell. Fascinating people from all different cultures and backgrounds. I wish I'd kept a journal of those years."

"But you do have your bird journals," Hugo reminded her. "That's your passion, Abby, and if you look hard enough I'm sure you'll see that your life is reflected in those recordings."

She smiled. "Maybe it is. I'll admit that I often find birds as interesting as people."

Hugo lowered the journal. "My two-week vacation on

Sparrow Island turned into twenty-six years, and I've enjoyed every moment of it. I feel God brought me here for a purpose. I've been blessed with good friends and the opportunity to share my love of nature with others."

Abby took a sip of her coffee, touched that she and her parents had been invited to share this special moment with Hugo. His anniversary had meaning for her too. If he hadn't come here and built the conservatory she might not have found such fulfilling work, as well as the chance to spend so much precious time with her family.

"I can't wait to see that new Rites of Spring exhibit you two have been working on." George leaned back against the sofa. "Although I'm not sure you can top the Wonderful World of Wings. That was my favorite."

"This one is even more expansive," Hugo told him, then looked over at Abby. "Your daughter's been working overtime for weeks to pull it all together. I think you'll be very impressed."

"It's going to incorporate everything about springtime on Sparrow Island," Abby added. "The birds, the wildlife, the marine life, the flora and the fauna. I think it will be wonderful."

Ellen's eyes widened. "That sounds like quite a challenge."

Abby met Hugo's gaze and they both smiled. "Absolutely," she concurred, "especially since the exhibit opening is only two weeks away."

Hugo walked over to the bookcase and replaced the journal. "We'll be working some long hours over the next two weeks to get everything ready, but I think it will be a wonderful exhibition. We're planning to go all out and make the opening a black tie affair and . . ." His voice trailed off as he stared quizzically at the row of journals.

"Is something wrong?" George asked him.

Hugo slowly fingered each volume, then shook his head

and began counting them again. "One of my journals seems to be missing."

"Missing?" Ellen echoed. "Are you sure?"

"Positive," Hugo replied. "I thought at first I'd gotten them out of order somehow, but one of my journals isn't here."

"Perhaps it's at your office," Abby suggested, knowing he sometimes wrote in his journal there.

"Maybe." Hugo sounded doubtful. "There has to be some reasonable explanation, although with the all the preparation for the display, I've been a little absentminded lately."

"Or it could have been stolen," Ellen ventured.

Abby blinked in surprise. "Stolen?"

Ellen lifted her shoulders in a small shrug. "There seems to be a petty thief on Sparrow Island. Several people have reported small items missing from their home or their yard."

Abby now remembered Mary mentioning something about a puzzling case Henry was working on, but she'd been so caught up in preparing the Rites of Spring exhibit that she hadn't really paid much attention to it.

"Are there any suspects?" Hugo asked.

Ellen shook her head. "Henry's investigating, but he hasn't come up with any leads yet."

"The oddest thing about it," George chimed, "is the items the thief is choosing to take. They're usually small things like a brooch or a compact mirror. Some of the things are of real value and others are almost worthless."

"That is strange," Abby said, then turned to her boss. "Maybe someone did steal your journal."

"I hope not." Hugo's brow furrowed with concern. "I probably left it in my office. I'll give my desk a thorough search in the morning."

"I hope you find it," Ellen told him.

"So do I." Hugo sat in the chair beside Abby. "Those journals are very important to me."

"They're the key to your past," George observed.

"That's true," Hugo mused. "Anyway, I have the most important memories locked in my heart. And I just want to thank you three for helping me make so many wonderful memories on Sparrow Island and for celebrating with me tonight."

Abby took his words to heart, realizing that she also had everything in life that truly mattered—her faith in God and the love of her family. One of her favorite Bible verses floated through her mind.

"And God is able to make all grace abound in you, so that in all things at all times, having all that you need, you will abound in every good work" (2 Corinthians 9:8).

Her gaze strayed once again to the bookcase and the empty spot in the organized row of Hugo's journals. An uneasy feeling stirred inside of her.

Hugo sighed. "I still can't believe there's a thief on Sparrow Island."

"I guess we'll all need to keep our eyes open for suspicious characters," Abby said.

"And watch out for each other," Ellen added as she reached for husband's hand.

That's what Abby loved most about living here. Friends and neighbors watched out for each other. They left their windows open at night to let in the gentle breeze and opened their doors to a stranger on the doorstep without trepidation.

Abby didn't want that to change. That's why she planned to do everything in her power to keep Sparrow Island a safe place to live.

CHAPTER ❧ TWO

On MONDAY MORNING, Abby arrived at the conservatory and discovered that one of the wildlife patients she was rehabilitating in her lab was missing.

The only sign that the mallard duck had been in the cage was one mottled brown feather in the bedding of cedar shavings. Now the door was standing wide open and there was no sign of the duck anywhere.

She looked around the laboratory, taking a mental count of her patients. The other three were all present and accounted for, including an orphaned baby rabbit, a small red fox with a broken leg and a horned owl with an infected claw.

Only the duck was missing.

Hugo stuck his head in the door. "Good morning, Abby. I thought I might find you here." Then he saw her expression. "Is something wrong?"

"I'm afraid so." Abby turned around to face him. "It looks like we have a duck on the lam. The mallard is missing from her cage."

Hugo looked from Abby to the empty cage and back again. "Missing? How in the world did that happen?"

"I don't know. Someone must have failed to latch the cage properly."

Abby hoped that someone wasn't Bobby McDonald, her ten-year-old neighbor who volunteered as a docent at the conservatory. She knew he'd been paying extra attention to the injured female mallard, even giving her the cute nickname of Quackers.

The duck had been found three weeks ago with a broken wing and brought to the conservatory. Until her wing fully healed, Quackers wouldn't be able to escape from predators in the wild or care for the eggs she would soon lay. The laboratory was the safest place for her.

There was a brooder box for newly hatched birds there as well as an incubator. The building even had its own generator in case of a power outage.

"Do you have time to help me look for her?" Abby asked Hugo.

He didn't even hesitate. "Of course. Where should we look first?"

Abby knew that if Quackers wasn't in the lab she might be in the tool room of the building where the grass mower and other machinery was kept. That room offered a lot more potential hiding places than the lab.

"She's probably looking for a private place to start laying her eggs." Abby led Hugo out of the laboratory. "The nesting instinct is pretty strong for a duck in her condition."

"Will she lay them soon?"

"Any time now. On average, a mallard duck lays one egg a day for about nine days, then incubates them for almost a month."

"That's fascinating," Hugo said. "I learn something new from you every day, Abby."

Hugo was one of the most educated men she knew, so she considered his words quite a compliment. "Almost as much as I learn from you. Mary enjoyed the Peking Dust, by the way."

He smiled. "I'm glad to hear it."

"Did you find your journal yet?"

He shook his head, emitting a weary sigh. "I turned my office upside down when I got to work this morning, but there's no sign of it anywhere. I can't imagine where it could be."

Disappointment seeped through Abby. She'd been hoping there was a simple explanation for the disappearance of Hugo's journal. He was so organized that there was little possibility he'd lost it.

They walked toward the tool room. A whiff of diesel fumes greeted them when Hugo opened the door. He flipped on the light, illuminating a bevy of dark and cozy hiding places for an expectant duck.

There was a workbench on the far side of the room with all kinds of equipment and open storage bins in between. The concrete floor was well-swept, revealing a few dark oil stains absorbed into the porous surface.

There were three cans of paint on top of the workbench along with assorted brushes and other tools. Abby knew that handyman Rick DeBow had volunteered to give the entryway of The Nature Museum a fresh coat of paint in preparation for the opening of the Rites of Spring exhibit.

"Do you see any sign of the mallard?" Hugo asked, looking around.

Her gaze slowly swept the room. "No, but perhaps Rick saw her when he arrived this morning."

"He's prepping the entryway for painting right now," Hugo said. "I just spoke to him a few minutes ago, but he didn't mention anything about a duck. I'm sure he would have said something if he'd seen her in here."

Hugo was right. Abby just hoped that Quackers hadn't found her way outside. That would make catching her even more difficult, if not impossible. Just attempting to recapture her could further aggravate the duck's wing injury.

Hugo moved a stack of wooden pallets that would make a perfect hiding place for a duck. As the wood scraped against the concrete floor, Abby saw a flash of feathers in the far corner of the room.

Tapping Hugo's shoulder to get his attention, she held up a finger to her lips, indicating the need for silence.

Then she pointed toward the corner where she'd glimpsed the duck.

Hugo nodded in understanding, then crept toward the tool room door, closing it silently to keep the duck from escaping.

Abby carefully picked up a canvas drop cloth from the workbench, then moved slowly toward the corner. She didn't want to startle the duck or stress her any more than was absolutely necessary.

Hugo followed quietly behind Abby, his Italian leather shoes not making a sound on the concrete floor. As Abby inched closer, she could see the top of the duck's head bobbing up and down. It looked to her like Quackers was eating something.

Abby gently dropped the cloth over the duck, then bent down to scoop Quackers up in her arms. The duck squawked in protest, but her broken wing didn't allow her to put up too much of a struggle. Abby cradled her carefully, providing just enough pressure so the duck couldn't injure herself trying to escape.

"Looks like we interrupted her lunch." Hugo picked up a ripped brown paper sack with Rick DeBow's name on it. Half of a bologna sandwich tumbled out onto the floor, along with a dill pickle and a small, unopened bag of potato chips.

Abby quickly perused the contents, assuring herself that there was nothing in the lunch sack that could hurt the duck's digestive system. "Looks like Rick will have to eat out this afternoon."

"I'll break the news to him," Hugo replied as they walked toward the door, "and offer to buy him lunch since he's painting the entryway for us."

Then he turned to face her. "Oh, that reminds me. I offered the caretaker job to a man named Wallace Sibley. He seemed to be the most experienced of the applicants and will start work tomorrow. Now Rick will have some help finishing that paint job."

Hugo had talked to Abby about hiring a part-time caretaker to do some minor upkeep and lawn care for the conservatory. "Thanks for letting me know. I'll keep an eye out for him so I can introduce myself."

"Do you need any help putting the duck back where she belongs?"

"No, I can do it." Abby shifted the bundle in her arms. "Although I may stay here awhile to make certain she's all right."

Hugo nodded. "I'll be available to help you with the display this afternoon. I'm free this evening as well if you'd like to work on it."

Abby shook her head. "I already promised Mary that I'd attend our book club meeting tonight. I've been so busy preparing for the exhibit that I missed last month's meeting."

Hugo's blue eyes sparked with interest. "What book are you reading this month?"

"*Hawaii* by James Michener," Abby told him. "I've never read anything by him before and I really enjoyed it."

"He's one of my favorite authors." Hugo opened the door for her. "As a matter of fact, I have another one of his books in my office. Why don't you stop by before you leave today and I'll lend it to you. I'm sure you won't be disappointed."

"I'd like that," Abby replied, pleased by the offer. "Mary didn't enjoy the book as much as I did, but maybe she'll like this one better."

"I can almost guarantee it," Hugo promised.

They parted company as they left the building, Hugo off to break the news to Rick DeBow about his ravaged lunch and Abby to take Quackers back into the laboratory.

Bobby was waiting there for her when she entered the lab. "There you are! I thought you released Quackers into the wild without me."

Abby smiled at his concern. "I wouldn't do that, Bobby. Quackers isn't going to be ready to go back to the wild for quite a while yet, especially after her latest adventure."

Curiosity lit his hazel eyes. "What adventure?"

"I found her eating Rick DeBow's lunch in the tool room."

"How'd that happen?"

"The door to her cage was left open." Then another thought occurred to her. "By the way, Bobby, don't you have school today?"

He flashed a grin. "Nope. The teachers have to go to some kind of special workshop, so I'm free for the entire day."

Abby removed the drop cloth from Quackers, then placed her carefully in the cage. The duck squawked a bit, ruffling her mottled brown feathers before finally settling down.

"How'd the cage door come open?" Bobby asked, testing the latch.

"I don't know. Someone might have left it open. Either way, I'm sure it was an accident."

"It wasn't me," Bobby proclaimed. "I gave Quackers some water yesterday and added some seeds and grain to her feed trough, but I always doublecheck the latches just like you taught me."

Abby secured the cage door. "I'm glad to hear it. Let's check all the cages to make certain they're latched, okay?"

"Okay."

Bobby took one side of the laboratory while she took the other. Abby found herself wondering how the duck had gotten out of her cage. She trusted all the employees and volunteers at the conservatory and knew none of them would be careless around the wildlife. Perhaps Quackers had found a way to manipulate the latch herself.

"Hey, Abby?" Bobby called out.

She looked up to see him standing by an empty cage.

"What is it, Bobby?" she asked, walking over to him.

"Look at that." Bobby pointed at a large gold coin in the middle of the cage.

Perplexed, Abby opened the cage door and picked up the coin. There was fresh dirt encrusted on it, as if it had been dug out of the ground. Yet, no animal had been in this particular cage for weeks.

"Where did this come from?" she asked.

Bobby shrugged his thin shoulders. "Beats me. I didn't see it there the last time I cleaned the cage."

Abby rubbed her thumb over the surface, not recognizing the image or the odd writing. It was obviously a foreign coin of some kind and looked very old.

"What should we do with it?" Bobby asked.

"I don't know." Abby handed the coin to him. "Could you research it for me and see what you can find out about it? That might help us figure out who it belongs to."

He grinned, slipping the coin into the front pocket of his faded blue jeans. "Sure."

"Will you do me another favor, Bobby?"

"Of course."

"Will you keep an eye on Quackers while I work on the display this afternoon? I want to make sure she stays in her cage so she can recuperate."

"Will do," Bobby affirmed. "I'll watch her like a red-tailed hawk. Did you know they can see eight times better than us?"

"I sure did," Abby said with a wide smile.

"I just wrote a report about them for school," Bobby explained. "They're so cool."

Abby couldn't argue with him. Her fascination with birds had led her to a career in ornithology. Despite over thirty-five years in the profession, she still had things to learn about the magnificent creatures. And she enjoyed every minute of it.

After work Abby was considering how to include a red-tailed hawk in the Rites of Spring exhibit as she left The Nature Museum. But her thoughts scattered when a loud shout turned her attention to the small creek that ran along a trail on the conservatory grounds. She raced toward the shouting.

A young couple stood on the trail, obviously in some kind of distress. The woman gripped the man's arm for support.

Hurrying over to them, Abby could hear the man's voice more distinctly now. He was calling out over and over again, "Adam! Adam! Where are you?"

"What's wrong?" Abby shouted.

"Our son's missing," the woman gasped. "He's only two and

a half years old. We were taking a hike. One moment he was with us and the next moment he was gone."

Abby's pulsed quickened as she thought of the possible dangers to a young child alone in the wilderness. "Are you sure he's in this area?"

The father nodded. "He has to be here. We were on the trail near the observation deck when we lost him. But we've looked everywhere . . ."

Abby knew finding little Adam wouldn't be nearly as easy as finding the duck. The conservatory covered a lot of ground, much of it thick with trees and brush.

"What does he look like?" Abby asked the boy's mother. All her instincts from her former work on search-and-rescue teams were kicking into gear. "Tell me what Adam is wearing."

The woman bit her lip, her eyes flooding with tears. "He's got curly blond hair and big blue eyes. He's wearing a little pair of blue overalls with a red shirt underneath. And he's got tennis shoes on—bright red tennis shoes."

"Okay," Abby said, wondering if she should call the authorities before starting a search. She knew they didn't have any time to waste.

"Adam!" the boy's father cried out in anguish. "Adam!"

"Don't yell like that," the woman admonished him. "He'll think you're angry and will be scared to come out from wherever he's hiding."

But another distant shout made them all turn to see a man emerge from a thick grove of cedar trees holding a small boy in his arms.

"Adam," cried the young woman, racing toward them.

The little boy grinned, obviously thrilled with the adventure that had caused his parents such panic.

"I found him hiding underneath a bush," said the man, surrendering the boy to his relieved mother. "I'd heard you shouting the name Adam so I asked this young fellow if that was his name. When he said yes, I put two-and-two together."

"I don't know how we can ever thank you," the father said, reaching out to shake the man's hand. "I'm Brent Halverson. And this is my wife, Tina."

"And I'm Abby Stanton, Associate Curator at the conservatory."

"Gary Diggs," the man replied to all three. "Happy to be of service."

Abby sent a silent prayer of thanks to God that little Adam had returned safely to his parents.

"We need to give you a reward or something," Brent said, glancing over at his wife. Tina Halverson only had eyes for her son, cooing to him as she nuzzled her cheek against his soft neck.

"That's not necessary," Gary replied.

Brent turned to Abby. "Can you recommend a good restaurant on the island? The least we can do is give Mr. Diggs a gift certificate for his help."

"There are several good places to eat here," Abby replied. "Winifred's is the fanciest, but the Springhouse Café is very good and one of my favorites."

"No, really," Gary protested, "you don't have to do a thing. The fact that your son wasn't hurt is reward enough for me."

The young boy tried to wiggle out of his mother's tight embrace. "I want a cookie!"

They all laughed. "I guess that's our signal that it's time to go back to the hotel," Tina said. "We have to find some way to thank you, Mr. Diggs. Do you live on Sparrow Island?

He shook his head. "No, I'm on vacation here. If you want

to do something for me, just promise me that Adam here gets a cookie for dessert tonight."

The Halversons laughed. "All right," Brent said. "We will."

Abby watched them leave, then turned to Gary Diggs. "Thank you again for finding that little boy. I hope you enjoy your stay on Sparrow Island."

"I will," he said, then gave her a wave and took off down the path.

Abby walked toward her car, wondering what else might go wrong today. Quackers had escaped from her cage, Hugo's journal was still missing and little Adam Halverson had given his parents quite a scare when he'd disappeared. She was just thankful that he'd been found so quickly and was unharmed.

At least she could look forward to her book club meeting this evening. She was ready for a relaxing break after working so hard on the Rites of Spring exhibit.

CHAPTER ✿ THREE

ABBY DIDN'T EVEN MAKE it three blocks before trouble reared its head once more. Her car began to wobble a bit, then bounced along the street until she carefully braked to a stop.

Climbing out of the driver's seat, Abby rounded the car, then groaned when she saw the flat rear tire on the passenger side. Glancing at her watch, she knew she'd have to hurry if she and Mary wanted to make it to the book club meeting on time.

She gave her sister a quick call on her cell phone to let her know she was running late, then she opened the trunk. Abby dug through all her hiking gear and birding maps until she uncovered the jack and the spare tire. Lifting the tire out of the trunk, Abby rolled it along the ground, then let it drop near the flat tire.

Next, she retrieved the tire jack and positioned it under her car. That's when she noticed the grease stain on the sleeve of her blue nylon jacket. Swallowing a sigh, she took care not to transfer any grease to the rest of her outfit.

As Abby began to loosen the bolts on the flat tire with the lug wrench, she remembered the first time her father taught her how to change a flat.

She'd just turned sixteen and was very excited to start driving. George Stanton had explained that responsibility came with every privilege and if she wanted to drive the family car she needed to know how to take care of it.

So he'd shown her how to check the oil and the water level in the radiator, as well as the proper way to use the jumper cables to start a dead battery. Her father had saved the tires for last, showing her how to use a tire gauge to check the air pressure, then demonstrating how to change a tire.

When he was through, he watched while Abby changed a tire all by herself. She'd taken a long time, wanting to make certain she'd done it just right. Her father had been patient with her, offering suggestions when she asked for his advice.

She smiled at the memory as she used the jack to lift the tire off the ground. Many of the things her parents had taught her were still with her today. Best of all, Abby knew she could still go to George and Ellen Stanton whenever she needed their help or advice.

Abby finished removing all of the bolts from the flat, then knelt down by the tire to pull it off of the hub. On the first tug, her hands slipped off and she landed right on the curb.

"Need some help?"

She looked up to see Gary Diggs straddling a bicycle. "I sure do. Can you help me get this tire off? It seems to be stuck."

Gary wheeled his bike to the curb, then got off to assist Abby. "Let's wiggle it a little bit."

They both wiggled the tire and after a few moments, it slid off the hub. Gary picked it up off the ground. "I'll put it in your trunk for you."

"Thanks," Abby replied, reaching for the spare tire. She'd have to make a trip to Al's Garage tomorrow to get the tire fixed so another flat didn't leave her stranded somewhere.

"Here, let me take that," Gary said, lifting the spare out of her hands.

Abby didn't argue with him. She didn't want to get any grease on her pink blouse or gray slacks. Then she could just slip out of her soiled jacket instead of finding an entire new outfit to wear to the book club meeting.

"You seem to have a knack for coming to the rescue," Abby said, watching him fit the spare tire on the hub.

He smiled up at her. "I'm happy to be of service. In fact, this is a good opportunity for me to ask you some questions about Sparrow Island."

"I'll be happy to answer them if I can."

"Have you lived here long?"

"I was born and raised here," Abby replied. "After earning my degree in ornithology I took a job at Cornell and spent thirty-five years teaching there before returning home."

He picked up the lug wrench and began screwing on the bolts. "So how does working at the conservatory compare to teaching?"

"The jobs are quite similar, actually," Abby said. "I lead birding tours, so I can continue to teach. I'm involved with research as I was at the university and also do wildlife rehabilitation."

"So you don't regret coming back?"

She found it odd that his questions were about her and not Sparrow Island. "No, not at all. Why do you ask?"

He shrugged. "Just curious. After living in New York for so long it must have been quite a change."

"A happy change," she assured him, then decided to ask

some questions of her own. "Do you have family or friends vacationing with you? I hope I'm not keeping you from them."

"I'm exactly where I want to be."

It occurred to Abby that while Gary Diggs was good at asking questions he was even better at dodging them.

"Are you from the East Coast?" she asked him, hearing a faint Boston accent in his voice.

"Yes," he replied, looking surprised. "Massachusetts. In a place quite different from Sparrow Island. You must know everyone who lives here."

She laughed. "Just about. Everyone's very friendly around here."

"It certainly seems that way."

"So how long are you planning to stay?"

"It depends. This is really more of a working vacation for me than a pleasure trip."

"Oh?" Abby was intrigued. "What are you working on?"

"A mystery, actually." He finished tightening the bolts on the tire, then rose to his feet. "I'm a private investigator."

"Really?" Abby loved a good mystery, both in fiction and in real life. She'd done some amateur sleuthing herself and was intrigued to meet a professional. "And you're here on a case?"

"That's right." He pulled a handkerchief out of his pocket to wipe the grease off his hands. "And I don't intend to leave until I solve it."

Abby wondered what kind of case could possibly bring a private investigator from the East Coast to Sparrow Island. "Well, you've already solved one mystery by finding that missing little boy."

Gary smiled. "I wish all my cases were that simple. The one

I'm working on now involves another missing person, only he's an adult. His name is Howard Barnaby."

She pondered the name, then shook her head. "I don't think I've ever heard of him."

"That's because he's living here under an assumed name."

Abby blinked in surprise. "You mean he's in hiding?"

Gary nodded. "That's right. He's taken on a new identity. Now it's my job to ferret him out and bring him to justice."

Abby thought about the series of petty thefts her mother had mentioned at Hugo's dinner and wondered if there was a connection. "Are you sure this Howard Barnaby is on Sparrow Island?"

"Positive." Gary tucked the soiled handkerchief back into his pocket. "He's probably got everyone here fooled, just like a wolf in sheep's clothing. Nobody realizes there's a con man living among them."

"What exactly has this Howard Barnaby done?"

"He's been cheating lonely widows out of their money for the last twenty years."

Abby couldn't believe it. "I can't think of anyone who matches that description. There are only about twenty-five hundred of us living on the island, Mr. Diggs, and I know a great number of them. Nobody who cheated one of their neighbors could hide for long."

"Please call me Gary," he replied. "And Howard Barnaby is too smart to indulge in illegal activities in his own hometown. He travels to the mainland and preys on women there. Then he undertakes a long distance romance with them, making all kinds of promises and convincing them to send him money until he's bled them dry."

"Have you gone to the police about this?"

Gary shook his head. "I don't want to do anything that might spook Barnaby. I've been tracking him for too long to take the chance of him running off when I'm just about ready to spring the trap."

Abby still wasn't convinced that Gary Diggs would find this Howard Barnaby on Sparrow Island, but he seemed so sure of himself that it made her uneasy. Was it possible that a con man really was living among them? A neighbor? A friend?

She picked up the tire jack and lug wrench, placing them back in the trunk. "Do you have a description of this man?"

Gary sighed. "That's the tough part. He changes his appearance each time he goes on the hunt for another victim. All we know is that he's over fifty, about six feet tall and in good physical condition. Unfortunately, his hair and eye color change with each victim, as well as his style of dress and his background information."

Abby was surprised by the description, expecting Barnaby to be a much younger man. "When do you think he moved to Sparrow Island?"

Gary shook his head. "I don't know. The trail to his last victim led me to a post office box in Seattle. That's where I did some more digging until I ended up here."

"Maybe there's some kind of mistake."

He snorted. "I wish that were true, Abby. Unfortunately, all the facts are starting to add up. Howard Barnaby is a charming man who likes to prey on lonely widows with too much time and too much money on their hands."

"How does he do that?"

"He befriends them," Gary explained. "Then he asks them to invest in some phony investment scheme. By the time they figure out the truth, he and their money are both long gone."

"That's terrible," Abby exclaimed, saddened that anyone would take advantage of vulnerable people.

Gary picked up his bike. "I've been on Barnaby's trail ever since the discovery that he defrauded one of my neighbors, a lovely woman named Vanessa Ellsworth. Her poor family didn't realize that he'd bilked her out of everything until she passed away and the will was read. That's when they asked me to step in and investigate."

"So this is a personal mission," Abby observed, "as well as professional."

"I'm determined to find Howard Barnaby," Gary proclaimed, "and finally bring him to justice. Maybe you can help me."

"Me?" Abby blinked at him in surprise. "How can I help?"

Before he could reply, a car drove up beside her. Inside was Rick DeBow. He rolled down his window. "Do you need any help, Abby?"

"No, thank you, Rick," Abby called out. "The spare tire's already on, thanks to Mr. Diggs here, and I'm ready to go."

"Okay." He gave her a wave. "Have a good night."

"You too," she said, waving to him as he pulled away and headed down Primrose Lane.

Gary watched the car drive off until it was out of sight, then he turned back to Abby. "I don't want to keep you, but . . ."

"Yes?"

"Well, Abby, you might be just the person who can help me unmask Howard Barnaby."

After all the assistance Gary had provided for her today she could hardly refuse him. "I'll certainly do anything I can."

He smiled with relief. "That's what I was hoping you'd say."

"What do you need?"

He hesitated a moment, then took a step closer to her. "I need you to tell me everything you know about Hugo Baron."

Her jaw sagged. "Hugo?"

He nodded, lowering his voice a notch. "I believe he's Howard Barnaby."

"That's impossible!" Abby tried to gather her thoughts. "If you knew everything he's done for Sparrow Island, I'm sure you'd realize that Hugo's the last man in the world anyone could ever suspect of such a thing."

"But don't you see?" Gary countered. "That's how he lures people. He *seems* like such a good and generous man. Then after he earns his victim's trust, he uses it against them to get what he really wants."

"You're wrong," Abby said adamantly, her defense bringing a hot flush to her cheeks. "Hugo Baron's a good, generous man, period."

Gary sighed. "But where'd he get the money to be so generous? What do you really know about his past? Can you tell me where he lived? How he earned his money?"

His questions didn't shake her faith in her boss.

"Hugo's a renowned naturalist," Abby replied, "as well as an intelligent and resourceful man. I'm sure he'll tell you everything you want to know if you just ask him."

"All in good time," Gary said. "I'm still gathering evidence."

The arrogance in his tone grated on her. Gary Diggs made a good first impression, but the more she talked to him, the more uncomfortable he made her.

"I should go," Abby said, moving toward the driver's door of her car.

"Yes, I've kept you long enough." Gary swung one leg over his bike, then balanced himself by setting both feet on the ground.

Despite her irritation, Abby knew she couldn't let him go without thanking him. "I appreciate your help with my flat tire."

"Glad to be of service." He pushed off the ground and pedaled closer to her. "I know it's hard to hear bad news about a friend, but all I ask is that you be cautious. I don't want Howard Barnaby to hurt you too."

"I'll be fine," she assured him, certain he was mistaken about Hugo. The sooner he realized it, the sooner he could start looking for the real con man.

Gary pedaled off, whistling into the dusk. Abby took a moment to gather herself, then she started up her car and headed for home.

Glancing at her watch, Abby groaned aloud when she saw the time. There was no way to avoid being late for their book club meeting now.

She pulled the car into the driveway and hurried into the house.

Her sister was ready to go, attired in a flattering navy blue suit with white piping and matching shoes. Mary always knew how to dress for every occasion and, unlike Abby, never seemed to have a hair out of place.

Finnegan, Mary's service dog, padded across the floor, his tail wagging when he saw Abby. Her sister had been lucky to get the golden retriever and Lab mix, since he'd been placed in retirement at one time. At eight years old, Finnegan was now part of the family and assisted Mary with things like opening or closing a door. Abby couldn't imagine what their life would be like without him.

"I'm sorry I'm so late." Abby ran her fingers through her wayward hair. "Not only did I have a flat tire, but there was a little boy lost on the conservatory grounds."

"Oh no," Mary exclaimed. "Is the boy all right?"

"Yes, he's back safe and sound with his parents." Abby reached down to pet Finnegan. "Although they were pretty shaken up by the whole thing. A tourist rescued him. Then that same man helped me with my flat tire."

"A real hero," Mary mused.

Abby wasn't so sure, but now wasn't the right time to discuss Gary Diggs and his accusations against Hugo. "If we leave now, we'll only be a few minutes late for the meeting. Do you mind driving?"

"Not at all," Mary replied. "I packed you a light supper to eat on the way to the library. It's in the fridge."

Abby smiled to herself as she shrugged out of her grease-stained jacket. She could always count on her big sister to take care of her, even after all these years. "Thanks, Mary."

"Don't mention it," her sister said, wheeling herself toward the garage. "Now let's get moving."

Abby retrieved the lunch box from the refrigerator, and followed Mary out to the white van that was specially equipped for her to drive.

Abby was tempted once more to tell Mary about her encounter with Gary Diggs, but she didn't want the news of the private investigator's suspicions about Hugo to cast a shadow on their evening out.

Abby told herself to just put it out of her mind. Gary Diggs was wrong about Hugo.

He had to be.

CHAPTER ❦ FOUR

W AIT UNTIL YOU HEAR the news!" Janet Heinz exclaimed as Abby and Mary entered the Sparrow Island library. Two long tables filled the center of the room. They were the last to arrive; the other six book club members were already seated around one of the tables.

Janet was the president of the Sparrow Island Book Club and worked as a secretary at the Little Flock Church. A petite woman, she had curly, reddish-brown hair and an infectious smile. She was a good friend of both Abby and Mary, as was fellow book club member Margaret Blackstock, the school secretary.

"What news?" Mary asked, rolling her wheelchair into the empty spot next to Janet.

"You won't believe it," chimed Edmonia Lewis as Abby sat down next to her. "You just won't believe it!"

Edmonia was Abby's hairdresser and owned the Silver Scissors beauty salon. Abby had rarely seen her so excited. The woman couldn't stop smiling.

Abby looked over at William Jansen, the editor of Sparrow Island's weekly newspaper *The Birdcall.* He was so busy jotting down notes on his legal pad that he didn't even seem to notice the late arrivals. She sensed his fervent writing had nothing to do with the book they were supposed to discuss this evening.

"What's going on?" Mary asked again as she looked around at the group members. It was obvious the book discussion hadn't generated this excitement. Each copy of *Hawaii* remained firmly closed on the table.

"Tell them, Janet," Sandy McDonald said. Bobby's mother taught English at the school and had a busy family life, but made time for the book club in her hectic schedule.

"I think Naomi should tell them," Janet replied. "After all, it's her news."

Abby looked at the head librarian, who cleared her throat as she rose to her feet. Naomi Yardley's slender frame and gentle manner belied her energetic spirit. She worked tirelessly to make their small library one of the finest in the area.

"I've received some wonderful news." Naomi's eyes sparkled with excitement. "Local authors Paul and Anne Riley have offered a very generous donation to build a new children's wing for the library."

The book club broke out in applause. The noise didn't disturb any patrons since the library closed at five o'clock on weekdays. Abby knew the new wing would be a welcome addition to Green Harbor. Though quite small, the library had an extensive collection of children's books, specializing in educational and resource books.

"I've already gotten a peek at the preliminary blueprints," Naomi continued, "and the new wing will be a lovely addition to our library. The Rileys have even planned a small, gated courtyard so the children can read on swings and benches.

"What a wonderful idea," Sandy said. "Reading is such a

vital part of a child's education. I always hope my students will make it a lifelong hobby."

Janet smiled. "I don't think you'll find anyone disagreeing with you here about the importance of reading. There's nothing I like better on a Saturday afternoon than immersing myself in a gritty mystery novel while sitting on my porch swing."

"My favorite spot is the easy chair in my living room," William said. "I can spend hours there reading a good book without even realizing how much time's gone by."

"Me too," Edmonia said, "although my favorite place to read is the bathtub. Believe me, when the water gets cold enough, I know it's time to stop."

The group laughed, then Margaret said, "I like to read in bed at night before I go to sleep. It's a great way to help me unwind from the day."

Several members started talking at once, the excitement about the new wing fueling their conversations. Then Janet clapped her hands together to get their attention.

"I think we can all agree that reading is an important part of our lives," Janet said. "Now I'd like Naomi to tell us if there's anything the Sparrow Island Book Club can do to help with the renovations."

Naomi pondered her request for a moment. "Actually, there might be. The Riley's generosity will give us a beautiful new wing and courtyard, but we don't have the resources to properly furnish it. All of our funds will go into buying books."

"As they should," William told her. "But there's no reason we can't raise money to buy furniture for the new wing."

Although gruff at times, William's dogged determination to fulfill his dream of becoming a newspaper man had earned him Abby's respect. He'd made his living as the CEO of Jansen

Essentials, a profitable company that manufactured diapers, along with other products. When he'd neared the age for early retirement, he'd chucked it all to move to Sparrow Island and buy the local newspaper.

Margaret's eyes widened. "We could buy cute kid-sized chairs and sofas for the new wing. Maybe even some padded window seats."

"That's a great idea," Sandy agreed. "But how will we raise the money?"

"We could hold a community fundraiser," Abby suggested. "The library serves everyone on the island. I think people deserve a chance to contribute to making it better."

"But what kind of fundraiser?" Mary asked, moving her wheelchair closer to the table. "Like a bake sale or something?"

"Or maybe a car wash?" Naomi added.

"We could sell something," Edmonia suggested, as members tossed ideas around. "I've always got kids coming into the shop trying to sell me magazines or candy to raise money for school activities."

"I'm not a good salesman," William said. "So I certainly don't want to go door-to-door to raise money. Besides, there are only eight of us."

"Selling things isn't one of my talents, either," Naomi admitted. "It makes me uncomfortable. I had a short and very dismal career as an Avon lady."

"We need to do something that's both fun and out of the ordinary," Abby said.

She looked around the room, certain that people with as many skills and talents as the members of this group could think of something unique to do to raise money for the library.

Then it hit her. "How about a talent show?"

"A talent show?" Janet echoed, tapping her chin with one finger. "Now that's an interesting idea."

"People could buy tickets to attend." Abby's enthusiasm for the idea grew the more she thought about it. "We could also ask for freewill donations at the door."

Sandy clapped her hands together. "We could sell refreshments too. I'd be happy to volunteer to bake something. I know I could talk the teachers at school into contributing some baked items too."

"Now we just need to find people to perform," Janet said.

"Mary could sing," Margaret suggested. She turned toward her friend. "You have such a beautiful voice. Everyone should hear it."

Mary shook her head, a look of horror on her face. "Oh no. I could never sing in public. I prefer to work behind the scenes."

Abby knew about her sister's long battle with stage fright. During a solo performance at a high school concert many years ago, Mary had forgotten the words to the song and stood frozen at the microphone. She'd never attempted to sing a solo in front of a large audience again, despite the pleas of her family.

"I don't want to perform, either," Edmonia said. "But I'd be happy to do all the hair and makeup for the performers."

Abby wondered if she could convince Hugo to perform his birdcalls. He was a natural at it. Like Mary, Abby preferred to work behind the scenes and was willing to fill in wherever needed.

Everyone started talking at once, with ideas bouncing back and forth between them. Then Janet held up her hands until the group quieted down.

"First, I think we should take a vote," Janet said. "All those in favor of hosting a talent show for the new children's wing of the library, raise your hand."

Eight hands shot up into the air.

"Wonderful!" Naomi exclaimed. "This is the icing on the cake."

After her harrowing day, Abby felt her spirits buoy at the unbridled enthusiasm of the group. She felt God's presence among them and knew that a community of believers could accomplish great and wonderful things when they put their hearts and minds together.

"Now I think we should elect a director," Janet suggested. "Then we can form committees to divide the workload."

"I nominate Janet," Mary said without hesitation.

Janet smiled at her friend. "Thank you for the vote of confidence, but I'm not sure I can handle the job all on my own. My plate is quite full at the moment."

"Why don't we elect two directors?" Abby suggested. "Then each one can be in charge of their own set of committees."

"Another good idea," Janet replied. "I nominate Mary as the other director."

The group cheered and Abby saw the happiness in her sister's eyes at the nomination. Mary had both the time and the talent to do the job well. Although she still owned Island Blooms, Mary had retired from full-time work, preferring a more supervisory role and leaving her floral shop in the hands of her capable assistant.

"I move that we close the nominations," Margaret said, who knew about *Robert's Rules of Order* from attending monthly school board meetings, "and elect Mary Stanton and Janet Heinz by unanimous decision."

"I second the motion," Edmonia said.

Margaret looked around the group. "All in favor, say *aye*."

A chorus of *ayes* affirmed the election of the two codirectors.

Abby was thrilled for her sister and knew Mary would enjoy working with her close friend on this project.

William cleared his throat, drawing Abby's attention. As she looked at him a startling thought popped into her mind.

Could William be Howard Barnaby?

The fact that she even considered it as a possibility surprised her. Yet, he fit the description that Gary had given of Barnaby: a man in his late fifties or sixties who had moved to Sparrow Island without any prior connections here.

Her mind wandered to other men on the island who also fit Barnaby's description. Handyman Rick DeBow. Town councilman Keith Gordon. Harbormaster Duncan Grady. All possible suspects, yet she didn't want any of them to be Howard Barnaby.

Abby shook the disturbing thoughts out of her head and focused on what William was saying.

"If we're going to pull this off, I think we should consider meeting here weekly." William looked around the group. "After all, putting on this talent show's going to be a lot of work."

Janet smiled. "That's a good idea, William. We're all in this together and a weekly meeting will give us a chance to coordinate with each other." She turned to Mary. "Maybe we should set up the committees tonight."

Mary nodded. "Sounds good to me. Edmonia's already volunteered for the backstage committee. She can prepare the performers to go onstage."

"I'll volunteer for the refreshment committee," Sandy said.

"We'll also need to nail down a location," Janet reached for a sheet of paper. "Finding a place to hold the talent show should be at the top of our list."

"I can do that," William volunteered. "I'll make sure to look for a place that will waive any rental fee for a good cause."

During the next fifteen minutes they came up with three more committees: performer recruitment, ticket sales and publicity.

"Speaking of refreshments," Margaret said, rising out of her chair. "I have a feeling we're not going to get to our book discussion of *Hawaii* this evening, so I'm going to go ahead and set out the cookies and coffee."

Abby smiled to herself when she thought about how late she'd stayed up last night to finish the book, but she didn't regret it. She loved all the energy that a group of people could generate when they came together in pursuit of a common goal.

She closed her eyes, giving a silent prayer of thanks for living in a community that cared enough to make a better life for everyone.

When she opened her eyes she saw the platter of cookies set out on one of the long tables in the center of the library.

As she got up to fix herself a plate, Abby heard William volunteer to head up the publicity committee. Her thoughts drifted again to the possibility that he could be a con man.

No. Impossible. Not only did she like and trust him, but she wouldn't describe his personality as charming. He could be a little crusty, especially when he was in serious pursuit of a story.

Gary Diggs had been adamant that Howard Barnaby was living on Sparrow Island. If he was right, that meant there was an imposter among them. Someone who took advantage of vulnerable people and hid his real identity.

The private investigator thought Hugo fit that description, but Abby knew better. So why couldn't she shake the feeling that disaster was just ahead?

Her father called what she was feeling internal radar. He'd told her sailors could sometimes sense an impending storm. Her own internal radar told her that she hadn't seen the last of Gary Diggs.

Edmonia moved beside her, walking with an extra spring in her step. "There's no better combination than a cup of hot coffee and an oatmeal cookie."

"I like them too," Abby replied, noting that something seemed different about her hairdresser, although she couldn't quite put her finger on it.

"In fact," Edmonia shot her a mischievous smile, "these cookies look so good I think I'll have two."

"I'll join you." Abby picked up another cookie, sensing the excitement about the fundraiser. She could tell by the way everyone was chattering that it was going to be a long and fruitful meeting.

"This is so much fun," Edmonia said, pouring them each a cup of coffee. "That's what I love about spring. It's full of new possibilities."

Abby took the Styrofoam cup Edmonia handed her, wondering what possibilities might be in store for Hugo if Gary Diggs pursued his investigation. Throughout the rest of the meeting, her mind kept wandering as she thought of her conversation with the private investigator and his insinuations about Hugo.

ON THE WAY HOME later that evening, Mary couldn't stop talking about the talent show.

"Just think, Abby, of how much fun it'll be. A place for everyone to get together and display their talents."

"I'm excited too." She leaned back against the passenger seat as Mary drove the van back to the house.

"What's wrong?" Mary asked her.

Abby turned to her sister. "What do you mean?"

"You haven't been yourself since you came home from work tonight. You seem . . . distracted."

"I'm fine," Abby assured her, torn between the wish to confide in someone and the hope that she could keep Gary Diggs' investigation a secret.

"You know you can tell me anything," Mary said gently. "You can trust me, Abby."

The words brought tears to Abby's eyes. So many times while living in New York she'd only relied on herself, not wanting to burden her family with her daily troubles. Now that she was home she needed to remember that love was never a burden.

"I met a private investigator today," Abby began.

"Really?"

"Yes. He's looking for a con man named Howard Barnaby who's living here on Sparrow Island under an assumed name."

Mary glanced at her. "I can't believe it."

"Neither can I," Abby replied. "The private investigator's name is Gary Diggs and he seems absolutely certain that this Barnaby character is living here, although he doesn't know how long he's been here. It could be months or years."

Mary slowly shook her head as she turned into the driveway. "Can you imagine finding out that someone you know and trust is a con man with a fake name?"

Abby took a deep breath. "He thinks Hugo is Howard Barnaby."

"Hugo Baron?" Mary pulled the van into the garage, then cut the engine before turning to her sister. "No wonder you haven't been yourself tonight. How can he possibly suspect Hugo?"

"I don't know," Abby admitted. "He claims to have evidence and told me he's in the process of gathering even more. Nothing I said seemed to convince him that he was wrong."

Mary reached for her hand, giving it a squeeze. "Hugo isn't a con man."

"I know," Abby said, but she felt so much better hearing her sister say it. That was the worst part of Gary's accusation. He'd made Abby begin to doubt her friend.

"You need to tell Hugo about this," Mary said. "He deserves to know there's someone on Sparrow Island investigating his past. That way he can clear up any misunderstandings, and this Mr. Diggs can start searching for the real culprit."

Abby realized her sister was right. Hugo did deserve to know the truth—no matter what the consequences. "I'll tell him first thing in the morning."

CHAPTER ❦ FIVE

ABBY DIDN'T SLEEP WELL that night, rehearsing in her dreams how she'd tell Hugo about the allegations Gary Diggs was making against him. She awoke with a headache that stayed with her throughout her morning devotional and cup of hot tea.

She even found herself grateful for the detour to Al's Garage on her way to work, though the delay wouldn't make it any easier for her to tell Hugo about the private investigator.

Al's Garage was located on Municipal street and serviced all types of cars. The owner, Al Minsky, was a man who loved automobiles. At forty, his light brown hair was balding on top, and he always seemed to be smiling.

The place smelled of oil and paint, an acrid combination that made Abby wrinkle her nose when she first walked inside the service area. But she soon adjusted to the smell and waited for Al to finish talking to another customer.

"Hey, Abby," he said, wiping the grease off his hands as he walked over to meet her. "What can I do for you?"

"I have a flat tire that needs to be fixed," she said, taking him to the car. She'd already opened the trunk for him.

"You sure do." Al pulled the flat tire out of the trunk of her car, then emitted a low whistle. "Wow, this one's a doozy." He examined the deflated tire. "Did you run over a spike or something?"

Abby shook her head. "I have no idea what happened, Al. It just went completely flat on me when I left work yesterday."

He ran his hand slowly over the thick rubber treads. Al specialized in foreign cars, but could fix anything with four wheels. "Didn't you just buy a new set of tires three months ago?"

"Yes," Abby replied. "That's why I was so surprised when this one went flat. Do you think you can fix it?"

"Nope. Look at this slice." He pointed out a long gash in the rubber. "Have you been doing some off-road driving, Abby?"

His question surprised her "Never. I always keep my car on the road, although I'll admit to pulling over once in a while to hike a trail or two."

"*Hmmm.*" Al stared at the tire, his brow crinkled in puzzlement. "Then I don't know how to explain this. I'll send it into the tire manufacturer and have them take a look at it. Since your tires are still under warranty, it shouldn't cost you anything to replace this one if it's defective."

She trusted Al's instincts. He and his wife had moved to Sparrow Island about twenty years ago and had two children. Al was gifted when it came to cars. Abby couldn't ask for a better mechanic.

He checked the spare tire for her to make sure it was properly secured and balanced before sending Abby on her way.

A few minutes later, Abby pulled into the parking lot of the conservatory, her stomach tied in nervous knots. She still wasn't looking forward to telling Hugo about Gary Diggs. Images of his possible reaction to the news fluttered through her mind. Would he be angry about such an accusation? Amused? Upset?

Whatever his reaction, Abby knew Hugo would accept what she had to say with the grace and dignity that had earned her respect from the first time they'd met.

Abby swallowed a sigh as she climbed out of the car, the March sun warm on her face. As with all unpleasant tasks, she knew it was best to face it immediately rather than put if off. So she walked into The Nature Museum and headed straight for Hugo's office—only to find that his door was closed. That was unusual. Hugo always left his door open, ready to welcome staff and visitors alike into his office. Glancing at her watch, she noticed that it was well past the time that he usually arrived for work.

Abby stood in the hallway, wondering if Hugo was involved in a meeting or perhaps an important telephone call. She didn't want to interrupt him, but recognized the temptation to delay telling him about Gary Diggs. If Hugo was busy she could make an appointment with him to come back at a later time.

She tapped lightly, then opened the door. The man standing at the bookcase wasn't Hugo. In fact, she'd never seen him before.

"Hello," he said, holding a feather duster in one hand. He wore blue coveralls and a friendly smile.

"Hello," Abby replied. "You must be Mr. Sibley."

"That's right, but all of my friends call me Wallace." He walked over to shake her hand. "I'd be pleased if you'd do the same."

"Nice to meet you, Wallace. I'm Abby."

His smile widened. "As in Dr. Abby Stanton?"

"That's me."

"Well, this truly is a pleasure. I've heard that you know everything there is to know about birds."

She blushed at the compliment. "Not everything, but I do love to study them."

"I've been looking at all the displays and stuff you have around here while I clean. Sure helps make the work go faster."

"I'm glad to hear it," she replied, then remembered the reason she'd come here. "Have you seen Mr. Baron?"

He shook his head. "Nope. Haven't seen him yet today."

"Well, I'll let you get back to your work." Abby headed for the door. "If you ever have any questions or concerns, just track me down and I'll be happy to help if I can."

"I appreciate that," he replied, applying the feather duster to the bookcase once more.

As she left Hugo's office she met Wilma Washburn in the hallway. Wilma was the conservatory's receptionist and general go-to gal.

"Are you looking for Hugo?" Wilma asked.

"Yes, I am. Have you seen him?"

"He won't be in this morning." Wilma brushed back a loose strand of her thick gray hair. Her Native American heritage was reflected in her dark eyes and smooth complexion.

"He called earlier to say he's got business on the mainland," Wilma continued, "and won't be back until sometime this afternoon."

"Oh." Abby was surprised he hadn't mentioned anything about the trip to her yesterday. Especially since they'd planned to work together on the Rites of Spring exhibit this morning.

"He did leave a message for you," Wilma said, pulling a memo sheet out of her pocket.

Abby quickly scanned it. *Abby, sorry about the last-minute trip. Something came up. I'll see you this afternoon. Hugo.*

The note was so vague and so unlike Hugo that it made her a little uneasy.

Wilma smiled as they walked down the hallway. "Maybe he went to visit Mrs. Downey."

"Who is Mrs. Downey?"

"The woman who calls here to talk to Hugo almost every day."

Abby felt a small pang at her words. Hugo had never mentioned a Mrs. Downey to her. "Perhaps she's interested in donating to the conservatory."

"Perhaps," Wilma said with a small shrug before they parted company.

Abby walked to her office, wondering what to make of Wilma's speculation. It seemed she thought Hugo and Mrs. Downey were romantically involved.

The words of Gary Diggs echoed in her mind. *He's been conning lonely women out of their money for years.*

She shook that ugly thought from her head. Abby never gave any credence to rumors. She'd learned early in her career how much damage they could do. During her tenure at Cornell a professor was accused of selling grades to students. The rumor spread like wildfire around the campus and resulted in angry calls from parents and alumni demanding his resignation.

When the truth finally emerged that a student had made up the rumor as retribution for a bad grade, the professor's reputation was in tatters. He resigned from Cornell, broken and bitter about the brutal assault on his character and good name.

She slipped into her lab coat, then headed for the laboratory to catch up on some research work and check on Quackers.

At first glance it seemed the mallard hadn't suffered any ill effects from her escapade yesterday. But a closer examination caused her some real concern. Quackers didn't move when Abby opened the cage door and reached for her. The duck acted listless, her dark eyes glazed and her brown head drooping.

Abby carefully lifted the duck out of the cage and checked her over. The broken wing seemed to be healing nicely and she could see no signs of infection. But Quackers' lethargy worried her and definitely indicated some kind of problem.

Turning her focus to the duck's cage, Abby looked for anything out of the ordinary. She thought about the gold coin Bobby had found in one of the empty cages yesterday and wondered if Quackers might have ingested some kind of foreign object.

That would explain the duck's uncharacteristic behavior. On top of that, the seeds and grain placed in the feed dish last night looked untouched. Abby gently smoothed her palm down the duck's long, narrow throat and over her gullet. She could feel a slight inflammation there.

"What'd you eat, Quackers?" she asked the duck, her tone soothing.

But Quackers wasn't talking—or quacking. The duck sat unmoving in her arms, a sure sign that something was wrong. Abby needed to figure out the problem before it got any worse.

Then she remembered the sack lunch.

She and Hugo had found the duck foraging through Rick's lunch yesterday. She thought the contents wouldn't have been harmful, but perhaps there had been something in there that Quackers ingested before they'd discovered her.

Abby gently placed Quackers back in the cage, then she left the laboratory and went in search of Rick DeBow. She found him standing on a step ladder in the entryway of the museum.

He was applying wide blue tape to the door frame to protect it from paint.

"Rick, may I talk to you for a moment?"

"Sure thing, Abby."

He climbed off his ladder, then pulled a rag from his pocket to wipe off his broad hands. Flecks of white paint speckled his green plaid shirt and faded jeans.

"What do you need?" Rick asked her.

"My runaway duck isn't doing very well this morning and I'm thinking she might have eaten something that wasn't good for her. Can you tell me everything you had in your lunch sack yesterday?"

He frowned. "You think she ate something that made her sick?"

"It's a possibility."

He tipped up the brim of his white painter's cap. "Well, let me think for a minute."

As Abby waited for his reply, she thought again about the fact that he fit the profile of Howard Barnaby. Rick was divorced and had moved to Sparrow Island after living the life of a high-powered stockbroker.

Abby knew he regretted the unethical business practices in his past, which was why he'd chosen to give it all up to become a handyman.

But maybe there was another reason.

Perhaps Rick had found an easier way to make money. The thought made Abby feel a little sick inside. She didn't like having suspicions about her friends and neighbors. Ever since Gary Diggs had told her about his search for a con man on Sparrow Island, seeds of doubt had begun to emerge in her mind about people that she'd known and liked for years.

"Abby?"

She blinked, realizing that she hadn't heard a word Rick had just said to her. "Oh, I'm sorry. Rick. I'm afraid I was daydreaming."

He smiled. "That's all right. My lunch wasn't too exciting. Just a bologna sandwich, a bag of potato chips and a dill pickle."

That's what Abby remembered seeing.

While not exactly the best diet for a duck, Abby couldn't think of anything in that description that would cause Quackers much gastric distress. She knew the duck hadn't touched the potato chips, since the bag was unopened when they found it. The sandwich was half-eaten and the dill pickle was intact.

"Are you sure that's all you had?"

"Yes," Rick said, then snapped his fingers. "No, wait a minute. Wilma gave me some of her homemade chocolate toffee when I came into work yesterday and I saved a piece for lunch. That was in there too."

Chocolate toffee.

Abby swallowed a groan. She had found the reason for Quackers condition. The caffeine and theobromine found in chocolate was highly toxic to birds, just like it was for cats and dogs. Because birds had a faster metabolism, it didn't take very much chocolate to make them sick.

"It was only a small piece," Rick said, seeing her expression. "A little chunk of toffee can't hurt a duck, can it?"

"Not the toffee," Abby told him. "But I'm afraid the chocolate can make any bird very sick. Even kill it. The duck has caffeine poisoning, but now that I know the cause of her illness, I can start treating her."

Rick breathed a sigh of relief. "So there's a cure?"

"Not a cure." Abby headed out the door, realizing she didn't have time to waste. "But I can give her something that might alleviate some of the symptoms and start her on the road to recovery."

"I'm sorry, Abby," Rick said, walking outside with her. "I had no idea . . ."

"It's not your fault," Abby assured him. "There was no reason to think a duck would get into the tool room and eat your lunch. I just wish I could figure out how she got out of her cage."

"Well, if there's anything I can do to help, let me know."

"I will," she promised, then turned toward the laboratory and walked quickly.

Quackers didn't look any better when Abby opened her cage. Abby understood the seriousness of the situation and the fact that the duck could still die from the ingestion of caffeine and theobromine. She treated the mallard with activated charcoal, then refilled the water bottle in the cage to rehydrate her as much as possible.

Now all Abby could do was wait.

Unfortunately, she had been through this before. In her work as a wildlife rehabilitator she was used to finding animals that had ingested something meant for humans. Too many people still littered, not realizing food that was perfectly safe for humans could be dangerous to animals.

Abby sat down on a stool, then grabbed a notebook to record Quackers' condition and catch up on all of her paperwork. She didn't want to leave the duck alone until she knew Quackers would recover.

"ABBY?"

The voice startled her. She looked up to see Hugo standing in the doorway of the lab. "Hello there."

"Do you have a minute?"

"Of course," she said, closing the notebook. "I was just looking for you." Then she glanced at the clock and realized hours had passed since she'd entered the lab. It was now late afternoon.

She'd worked right through lunch without even realizing it.

"Rick told me about the chocolate toffee," Hugo said, walking into the lab. "How's the duck doing?"

"She seems better," Abby replied, her gaze on the mallard's cage. Quackers was resting comfortably now and had even eaten a few pieces of grain.

"I'm glad to hear it." Hugo sat on the stool next to her. "I felt guilty for skipping out on you this morning after our plan to work on the display together."

"That's all right," she said, still wondering about his mysterious disappearance.

He hadn't offered an explanation yet, which only made her more curious. Hugo wasn't the secretive type.

"I've been in here for most of the day," Abby said, "so I haven't had a chance to work on the display myself."

Abby knew that she had to tell him about Gary Diggs, but his arrival in the lab had caught her off guard. She wanted to find a way to ease into the subject.

"How was your book club meeting last night?" Hugo asked her.

"Terrific. The library is receiving a donation to build a new children's wing and our book club decided to raise additional funds by hosting a talent show."

His blue eyes widened with delight. "That's wonderful news. Let me know if there's any way that I can help."

Abby nodded, still searching for the right words to tell him about Gary Diggs. She knew the longer she waited, the more difficult it would be. Better to just come out and say it.

"I met someone last night," she began.

"Oh? A new member of your book club?"

"No." Abby pushed away the notebook in front of her, hating this awkward pause between them. "The man I met is a private investigator. His name is Gary Diggs and he's here on a case."

She waited to see a reaction, but Hugo didn't flinch at the name. That told her he had no idea about the investigation or the suspicions against him.

"That's intriguing," Hugo said. "What's he investigating?"

She took a deep breath. "You."

Hugo stared at her. "Me?"

She nodded. "Mr. Diggs believes you're a con man living here under an assumed name."

"A con man," Hugo echoed, then pointed to himself. "Are you sure he means me?"

She found it just as difficult to believe. "Yes. Gary believes your real name is Howard Barnaby and that you scam lonely widows out of their money."

He tensed. "Is that so?"

The fact that he didn't instantly deny the charge made her uneasy. "He was hired by the family of a woman named Vanessa . . ."

"Ellsworth," Hugo finished for her. "So this is about Vanessa."

"Yes. He's here to find Howard Barnaby and recover the Ellsworth fortune."

Abby hated the suspicions arising in her mind now, but Hugo's reaction to the news about Gary Diggs wasn't at all what she had expected. Worse, Hugo did know Vanessa Ellsworth. That probably explained why Gary seemed so certain he'd found his con man.

Hugo cleared his throat. "I met Vanessa a few years ago in Massachusetts. She'd led a fascinating life, having grown up in Burma where her father was a diplomat. We kept in touch and she was quite interested in the conservatory. She made several generous donations before her death."

"Do you believe that's why her family hired a private investigator?" Abby asked him, relieved by the innocent explanation. "To get those donations back?"

He shrugged. "It doesn't make any sense. Why not contact me directly instead of hiring someone to come all this way?"

Abby agreed. Something strange was going on here. "Gary Diggs is convinced you're Howard Barnaby."

"Then I'll have to convince him otherwise," Hugo told her. "The conservatory can't afford to have an ugly rumor like that swirling around here. As the Curator of the Sparrow Island Conservatory, I must be above reproach."

Abby agreed, although she knew convincing Gary Diggs wasn't going to be easy—just like she knew rumors had a way of spreading before you could stop them.

She slid off her stool. "I have an idea."

"I can't wait to hear it."

She knew rumors could be as toxic to the human spirit as chocolate was to birds. So Abby intended to practice some preventative medicine. "I'll prove that you're not the con man."

Hugo arched a silver brow. "How do you intend to do that?"

"By finding the real Howard Barnaby."

CHAPTER  SIX

Abby knew that finding Howard Barnaby wouldn't be easy.

The worst part of the task involved considering all of her friends and neighbors as potential suspects. Some of them she'd known since she was a child. But if she wanted to clear Hugo's name, she had to consider every possibility.

Abby sat at the dining room table on Thursday evening, the aroma of fresh brewed coffee scenting the air. Tapping her pen against the table, she looked over the list she'd compiled of all the men she knew on Sparrow Island who fit some part of Barnaby's profile.

It was much longer than she'd expected, thirty names in all. That made her job of finding the con man all the more difficult.

Many on the list were her friends. Some were even members of Little Flock Church. All of them were people she knew and liked. People who would take offense if she walked up to them and asked if they had ever bilked a widow out of her money.

Worst of all, she hated to think that one of them might be Howard Barnaby, hiding behind a phony mask of respectability. The only thing that gave her comfort was knowing that while everybody had secrets, nobody could hide from God.

Bowing her head, Abby prayed for Him to give her the strength she needed for the challenge ahead. She ended her prayer just as the doorbell rang, signaling the arrival of Sergeant Henry Cobb.

He and Mary had a dinner date this evening, giving Abby the perfect opportunity to consult Henry about her investigation. She'd called him earlier in the day and asked him to stop by early so she could talk to him about the case. Now, as she rose to answer the front door, Abby found her palms damp with apprehension.

The doorbell rang again.

The one thing that Abby hadn't told Henry was that Gary Diggs suspected Hugo was the con man. She told herself it was because the assertion was ridiculous, but that wasn't the real reason. She didn't want Henry to look at Hugo in a different light or to think badly of him.

Maybe she wasn't giving Henry enough credit. After all, she'd told Mary about Gary's suspicions. Yet, somehow saying it aloud gave it more credence.

"Abby?" Mary's shout carried from her bedroom and into the living room. Though always punctual, Mary spent a lot of time making sure she looked just right for every occasion. "Can you get the door?"

"I've got it," Abby called back, wiping her hands on her slacks and taking a deep breath before she opened the door.

Henry stood before her wearing dark brown pants and a

crisp beige shirt on his stocky, six-foot frame. At sixty-two, he was quite a handsome man with a fringe of white hair around his balding pate and kind brown eyes.

"Hello, Abby," he said with a smile. "Nice to see you again."

"Hello, Henry," Abby stepped aside to let him in. "Thank you for coming by early this evening. I hope it wasn't any trouble."

"Not at all," he assured her. "The more time I get to spend here, the better. You two do a good job of making me feel right at home."

His words made Abby smile. Henry doted on her sister, and best of all, he made Mary laugh. As the San Juan County Deputy Sheriff, Henry took his job very seriously, but he enjoyed his leisure time as well. They'd all spent many an evening playing games together.

"Mary should be ready to go in just a few minutes," Abby told him as they moved into the living room. "Please have a seat. Can I get you something to drink? I've got coffee made."

"No, thank you. Mary and I are headed to the Springhouse Café, so I'll have a cup there."

A fire glowed in the hearth, warming the cool March evening. Finnegan lay on the rug in front of it, his silky fur gleaming a burnished gold in the firelight. The dog lifted his head as Henry approached, blinked once, then lowered it again and went back to his nap.

Henry sat down in the overstuffed chair, his favorite spot. Resting his elbows on his knees, he launched into the topic.

"I looked up the name Howard Barnaby in my police database just like you asked."

"And?"

"And his name isn't in there," Henry replied. "So either he's not really a con man or he just hasn't been caught yet."

"Thanks for checking, I appreciate it."

"You're welcome." Henry paused a moment. "Your phone call intrigued me, Abby. Con men and scam artists are some of the toughest criminals to catch. They skirt around the edge of the law and usually by the time the victim realizes he's been swindled the con man's long gone."

"So you're not surprised that Barnaby's name wasn't in the database?"

"Not really. That's why I went to the source."

Abby looked at him, confused by his words. "What source?"

"I tracked down Gary Diggs." Henry softened his expression with a smile. "I hope you don't mind, Abby, but if there's a con man on Sparrow Island I want to know about it."

"I'm glad you spoke to him," Abby said. "Did he happen to mention his prime suspect?"

"He did," Henry said softly. "And now I know why you're so concerned about this investigation."

Relief washed over her that Henry knew the truth. She'd told Mary, but hadn't wanted to spread Gary Diggs's suspicions around the island. That would only serve to make people start having doubts about Hugo.

Just like the doubts she was experiencing because of those ugly little seeds planted in her mind by Gary's insinuations. "It's ridiculous, isn't it?" Abby said, looking into Henry's eyes for confirmation. What she saw there troubled her.

"In my line of work, I have to consider every possibility." He sighed. "I know it's not easy, Abby, but all we really know about Hugo's past is what he's told us. I trust him and I'm sure you do too. But trust is the best weapon a con man can use against his victims."

Henry leaned back against the cushion. "Con men are masters of manipulation, Abby. That's why they're usually the last person you'd expect of such a crime. They use their charm and friendly personality to assure their victims they're harmless. This Howard Barnaby not only robbed his victims of their money, but of their trust and faith in their fellow man. Once you've been burned by a con man it's hard to trust anyone again."

Abby thought that was the worst crime of all. Money and material items could be replaced, but trust and friendship were priceless.

"I'm not sure we should trust Gary Diggs, either," she mused. "We don't know anything about him or this supposed evidence he's gathered against Hugo. He may be totally incompetent."

"That's true," Henry conceded. "I'm certainly not ready to make any judgments yet. As far as I'm concerned, Hugo's innocent until proven otherwise."

She breathed a sigh of relief at his words, the tension easing in her shoulders and neck. "I *know* he must be innocent, but it seems the only way to prove it is to find the real con man."

"And I'll be happy to help in any way I can," Henry assured her. "But I've got to tell you that it's not going to be easy. If this Barnaby fellow is in hiding somewhere on the island, he's not going to come out when people start asking questions."

She knew he was right. Yet, Abby didn't have any choice. If she couldn't find Barnaby, the least she could do was eliminate Hugo as a suspect.

"So far," Henry added, "I'm not convinced Gary Diggs has much of a case against Hugo. The only evidence he has so far is that Hugo spent a month in Massachusetts at the same time that Vanessa met Howard Barnaby."

"Is that it?"

Henry shrugged. "Gary claimed he has other evidence, but he refused to show it to me. Apparently, he doesn't want to do anything to tip Barnaby off and cause him to flee before he's ready to make a case against him."

"Then why tell me about his investigation?" Abby mused. "Surely he'd know that I'd inform Hugo."

Henry gave a slow nod. "That's true. I wish I knew the answer to that question. Perhaps this Howard Barnaby isn't the only one on Sparrow Island with something to hide."

Mary rolled her wheelchair into the living room, instantly capturing Henry's attention. "Hello, Henry."

He rose to his feet, his gaze fixed on her face. "Hello, beautiful."

Mary blushed at the compliment, though Abby agreed her sister did look beautiful this evening. Mary had a real talent for coordinating colors and fabrics that best suited her complexion. It was a talent that Abby was sadly lacking.

She preferred comfort over style, choosing to wear slacks and a blouse at work, and a sweatshirt and jeans when she explored the woods. Every once in a while, Mary persuaded her to be more adventurous with her wardrobe, though Abby had never quite achieved her sister's sense of style.

"You do look wonderful," Abby said, touched by the way Henry looked at her sister.

"Thank you." Mary set her small purse in her lap. "I heard you two talking in here. I hope I'm not interrupting."

"Not at all," Abby assured her. "I was just asking Henry for his advice about my search for Howard Barnaby."

Mary shook her head. "I still can't believe we've got a con man living on Sparrow Island."

"I know," Henry replied, "but in my line of work, I've seen

plenty of folks who look respectable on the outside but are rotten to the core."

Abby considered his words. "I think it's because they're empty inside. They turn away from God and seek out material things and cheap thrills to try and fill their life with meaning."

"But Hugo isn't like that," Mary said. "So even if this Mr. Diggs does make him the focus of his investigation I'm sure Hugo's got nothing to hide from any of us."

Abby wished she could be as certain. His behavior of late was a little strange, though nothing she could quite put her finger on. The frequent phone calls from Mrs. Downey concerned her too. While Hugo did like chatting with benefactors, he never spoke with them on a daily basis.

She looked at Henry, disconcerted by his silence. Perhaps as a member of law enforcement he needed to maintain his objectivity. Henry relied on evidence to solve crimes—the kind of evidence she needed to lift the shadow of suspicion that hung over Hugo.

"How do you think I should approach this?" Abby asked him.

"I know it's difficult to even think that Hugo might be guilty," Henry replied. "Unfortunately, it's sometimes necessary to conduct a criminal investigation by a process of elimination. If you want my advice, I think you should evaluate Hugo as you would a stranger, without the natural bias of friendship clouding your judgment."

"How's that even possible?" Mary asked.

Abby wondered the same thing. Yet, she knew that Henry had a point. If she wanted to clear Hugo's name, she'd have to conduct a thorough and objective investigation, even if it meant considering him as a suspect.

"I know it won't be easy," Henry said, "but Abby's got a

good head on her shoulders. Con man or not, if this Howard Barnaby's living on Sparrow Island, he won't be able to fool her for long."

Abby was touched by Henry's confidence in her. She just wished she felt as certain. According to Gary Diggs, Howard Barnaby had been conning people for several years. It was certainly long enough to perfect his nefarious craft and fool everyone he met.

Mary glanced at her watch. "We'd better go."

Henry rose to his feet. "Good luck, Abby. Let me know if I can be of any more assistance."

"Thanks," Abby said, then escorted the couple to the door. "You two have a good time tonight."

She watched them leave, her heart as heavy as the still night air. The last thing that Abby wanted to do was investigate her friends, look for unexplained holes in their lives or start questioning their integrity. Yet, she knew no other way to exonerate Hugo than to find the real Howard Barnaby.

Abby stepped outside, her gaze drawn to the clear night sky. A few twinkling stars peeked through the cloud canopy above her, reminding her that God always provided a light through the darkness. She needed to have faith that He would guide her path in her search for the truth.

The evening air smelled of rain and she saw lightning flash in the distance.

The sound of a door creaking open next door made her look toward the McDonald's house. She heard Bobby's footsteps bounding across the front lawn toward her and her heart lightened. His youth and exuberance always made her smile.

"Hey, Abby," he called out, hurdling over a small shrub to reach her. "I have a great idea for the talent show!"

Her smile widened. "Does that mean you're planning to perform?"

"For sure," he exclaimed, tugging on the tail of his red T-shirt. "A bunch of the kids at school are going to be there. We figure it's the least we can do for the new addition to the library. Plus, I think it's going to be fun."

"So do I." Abby was thrilled that the talent show was already generating publicity.

"So can you guess what I'm going to do?" Bobby said.

"What?"

He grinned. "I'm going to audition for the talent show as a juggler."

"A juggler?" Abby echoed. "I didn't realize you knew how to juggle."

"I'm not very good yet," he admitted. "My mom said I can't practice with anything breakable."

Abby stifled a giggle. The McDonalds had their hands full with Bobby. His quick wit and enthusiasm made him eager to try all kinds of new adventures. She knew Neil and Sandy couldn't be prouder of their young son.

"What made you decide to try juggling?" Abby asked him.

"Well, we had Hobby Day at school where a bunch of people came and showed us their hobbies. There was stuff like whittling wood and stamp collecting, along with this really cool juggler. He juggled these eight crystal glasses all at one time and even tossed a bunch of them behind his back."

"Wow," she replied, "that does take talent."

He nodded in agreement. "Then he taught us some of the fundamentals of juggling. I've been practicing ever since."

"Practice does make perfect," she chimed.

"I know," he said, then sighed. "But I didn't know it would be this hard. Mr. Danker said he learned how to juggle when he was about my age. Then he joined the circus and traveled all over the world before retiring and moving to Sparrow Island."

As far as Abby knew, she'd never met a Mr. Danker and was intrigued by both his former profession and his travels. From the sound of it, he might fit the profile of Howard Barnaby.

"Mr. Jordan was cool too," Bobby said.

"Who's Mr. Jordan?"

"He's a falconer. He even brought his falcon to school and showed us how he trained her." Bobby held up his arms and spread them wide. "Her wingspan was like *this big*."

Abby was intrigued to have a falconer on the island.

She knew the hard work, patience and dedication it took to train such a majestic bird.

Falconry was an ancient art involving long-winged hawks and had become a status symbol in medieval society. These days the practice was rapidly shrinking because it was difficult to find enough land for falconers to fly their birds.

"Sounds like an interesting Hobby Day," Abby said.

Bobby nodded. "It was great. I told Mr. Jordan about my report on red-tailed hawks and he said I could come and watch him train Calypso sometime. That's the name of his falcon. It's Latin or something."

"It's Greek," Abby told him, "and it means concealer." Abby found the falcon's name interesting and wondered if Mr. Jordan had something to conceal. Could it be possible that she had another suspect to add to her rapidly growing list?

"What does Mr. Jordan look like?"

Bobby seemed surprised by her question. "Just like a regular guy, I guess. He's got gray hair and he's as tall as my dad, but a lot older."

Abby nodded, realizing he fit the profile of Howard Barnaby as well. The problem was that too many men on Sparrow Island fit the profile. She wasn't sure how to narrow them down and didn't have the time or the means to investigate everyone, especially with the Rites of Spring opening right around the corner.

"You can probably come with me if you want to see Calypso," Bobby said. "All we have to do is take the ferry over to Lopez Island and find Mr. Jordan's house."

That eliminated Mr. Jordan from suspicion. Gary had specifically said that Howard Barnaby lived on Sparrow Island.

"I better go," Bobby said. "Mom told me I had to come right back and do my homework."

"Thanks for stopping by," Abby said, as he turned back toward his house. "I'm looking forward to seeing you juggle."

He flashed her a grin over his shoulder, then headed for home.

Abby watched him go, happy that he'd paid her a visit. Bobby had also brought her some useful information about a resident of Sparrow Island who fit the description of Howard Barnaby.

It was a description that was growing murkier by the day.

CHAPTER 🌹 SEVEN

ON FRIDAY, ABBY FOUND herself looking forward to her weekly lunch out with Janet Heinz at the Springhouse Café. She'd been so busy working on the Rites of Spring exhibit that she'd put her social life on the back burner. Now she was ready to enjoy a long lunch. Margaret would be there, too, which would give them all a chance to discuss their progress in finding volunteers for the talent show.

Margaret and Abby comprised the performer recruitment committee, though any book club member was welcome to recruit local talent for the show.

As she sat at the Springhouse Café waiting for her good friends to arrive, Abby was almost giddy with excitement. This was as close to the entertainment business as she'd ever gotten and she couldn't wait to mine the talent on Sparrow Island.

"Hello there, Abby."

She looked up to see Tina Halversen holding little Adam in her arms. Brent Halversen stood behind her, one broad hand on his wife's shoulder.

"Why, hello," Abby replied. "How nice to see you again. Have you been enjoying your vacation?"

"Very much," Tina replied. "This is our last day on the island, so we're making the most of it."

"Well, you picked the perfect place for lunch."

The couple glanced at each other. Then Brent said, "Actually, we were planning a picnic, but Mr. Diggs called and reminded us of our offer to buy him a meal, so we agreed to meet him here."

Abby sensed that the family would have preferred to spend their last day on the island alone, but were too polite to tell Gary.

"We owe him so much for finding Adam," Tina said quickly, as if worried they sounded ungrateful. "It's the least we can do."

"That's very kind of you," Abby said. "I hope you enjoy your meal."

"I'm sure we will," Tina replied. "It was nice seeing you again."

"You too." Abby watched them head for their table, as Ida Tolliver approached her.

"Hey, Abby." The pretty blonde wore the standard waitress uniform of a white top with navy khakis and white leather sneakers. "Is Janet meeting you for lunch today?"

"Yes," Abby replied. "Margaret's coming too. We're planning the talent show."

Ida's violet eyes widened. "I've heard about that. It should be fun."

Abby folded her hands on the table. "We're looking for volunteers if you're interested in performing."

Ida blushed, laying one hand on her chest. "Me? I don't

have any talent—except for finding trouble, and that's a talent I'm trying to overcome."

Abby knew Ida was only half-joking. She didn't have the best taste in men and had even gotten involved with a drug dealer a while back. But she was a nice young woman and was learning the value of community. Ida had recently joined Little Flock and her new church family had taken her under their wing.

"Well, just think about it," Abby told her. "If you change your mind, let me know."

Ida smiled as she placed the menus on the table. "That's not going to happen. Even if I did have a talent, I most definitely have stage fright. I'd freeze in front of all those people staring at me."

Janet and Margaret arrived at the table, changing the subject from stage fright to the café's noon special. After they placed their orders, the three women began planning the strategy of the talent committee.

"I think we should send out letters," Margaret said, "inviting people to an audition. Then we could select our performers all in one evening."

Janet took a sip of her water. "We can't afford a mass mailing. Besides, what if no one showed up?"

"I guess you have a point." Margaret wrinkled her nose. "Does that mean we need to go door-to-door looking for volunteers?"

Abby had an idea. "Why don't we advertise for performers in *The Birdcall*? It won't cost that much, and we can spread the word about the talent show at the same time. I know William's writing an article about it, but a little reinforcement never hurts."

"That's true," Janet said. "If you both agree, I'll contact the paper this afternoon and place the ad. Do you mind if I include your phone numbers as a contact?"

"Not at all," Margaret replied and Abby nodded her agreement.

Ida arrived with their orders, setting a Caesar salad in front of Janet and the noon special of crab bisque before both Abby and Margaret.

"The soup looks delicious," Janet said, then glanced up at Ida. "I think I'll take a small cup to go with my salad."

"I'll bring it right out," Ida said, heading off toward the kitchen.

Margaret smiled. "I guess great minds think—and eat— alike."

Janet picked up her fork. "That's why I assigned the two of you to the talent committee. I knew you'd give us a nice variety and only quality performers."

Abby hoped she and Margaret wouldn't disappoint her. The performers would be the foundation of the talent show and so far they had a blank slate except for Bobby's juggling act. This made her consider another possibility.

"Maybe we should start asking around for volunteers, as well as advertising in the newspaper," Abby said. "We don't have to go door-to-door necessarily, but if we run into someone who'd like to perform, we can sign them up."

"I've already been trying that," Margaret said, "but I haven't gotten any takers yet."

"Well, we can put Bobby McDonald down for sure," Abby told them. "He's trying to learn the art of juggling in time for the show."

Margaret crumbled a soda cracker into her bisque. "Do you

realize that our talent show's only two weeks away? The time's just flying by."

"That's why we may need to start personally recruiting performers," Abby said. "After all, *The Birdcall* doesn't come out until next Wednesday. That's five days with no progress for our committee."

"You have a point," Margaret agreed. "We can't wait too long to start lining up quality performers."

Ida returned with a cup of crab bisque for Janet. "Here you go."

"Thank you," Janet said as the waitress set it in front of her. "It looks wonderful."

"Wait until you taste it," Margaret chimed.

Janet picked up her spoon. "Look, you two are in charge here so feel free to take whatever action you think is necessary."

"I'd like to talk to Mary again," Margaret mused, "just to see if I can convince her to sing in the talent show. A voice like hers needs to be heard."

Abby dabbed at her mouth with her napkin. "I know you mean well, Margaret, but I'm positive Mary won't change her mind."

Margaret sighed. "That's a shame."

"I'm sure we can find plenty of volunteers," Abby said, "although we may have to gently twist a few arms along the way."

Janet cleared her throat. "I wouldn't mind a little arm twisting."

Abby looked at her. "You want to perform?"

"Well, I've been working on a piece for a while now called 'Whispering Hope.'" A reminiscent smile curved Janet's lips. "It's one of my mother's favorite songs."

Margaret's brow furrowed. "I didn't know you played the piano."

Janet laughed. "Oh, no, I can't play a note. I'm talking about singing a solo."

Ida arrived with a pitcher of iced tea to refill their glasses. "Is there anything else I can get you, ladies?"

Abby glanced at her friends, then shook her head. "No thanks, Ida. I think we're fine. We may be here awhile though."

"Stay as long as you like," Ida told them. "The lunch crowd's winding down so we have plenty of room."

As soon as Ida left the table, Margaret leaned forward and whispered in a low voice, "Janet, you can't be serious."

"What do you mean?" Janet asked her.

"About singing a solo."

Janet laughed. "Of course I'm serious. I know I've never done it before, but I think it would be a nice tribute to my mother. And I'm certain that I can help Mary direct the talent show and perform in it at the same time, if that's what you're worried about."

Margaret shook her head. "It's not that."

"Then what?" Janet asked her.

"Oh, never mind." Margaret picked up her glass and took a long sip.

Abby didn't know what to say, though it seemed obvious that for some reason Margaret was against Janet's offer to sing at the talent show.

Judging by the flush creeping up Janet's neck, she'd come to the same conclusion. "You don't think I can sing?"

"Of course I do," Margaret replied. "It's just that . . ."

"What?" Janet prodded.

Abby heard the tension in Janet's voice and something told

her this wasn't going to end well. She opened her mouth to intercede, but Margaret spoke first.

"I just don't want you to embarrass yourself," Margaret said hastily. "Remember that time you sang a solo in church and your voice cracked? None of us minded because we all love you. But what if that happens onstage in front of a huge audience? It would be terribly embarrassing."

"That was over two years ago," Janet explained, "and I had a horrible cold that day. The only reason I sang was because I'd made a commitment to the choir and Rev. Hale."

"I know," Margaret said contritely, "I'm just telling you as a friend."

"Well, then I guess I should thank you." Janet turned her attention to her soup, refusing to look at either Abby or Margaret.

Tension crackled in the air as the three of them ate silently together. Abby searched for something to say to defuse the situation.

"Bobby's so excited about his juggling act," Abby began. "He's been practicing with tennis balls and apples and all sorts of things."

Margaret gave her a wan smile. "He's such a cutie."

Janet sat with her gaze still on the soup in front of her, though she'd hardly touched a bite.

Concern creased Margaret's brow. "Are you upset with me?"

Janet sniffed, placing her spoon on the table. "I'm not upset. I'm hurt."

"Well, don't be," Margaret said. "You can sing if it means that much to you. I'll put you down on the list."

"No, thank you," Janet said stiffly. "I've changed my mind."

"I'm sorry I ever said anything about it," Margaret said.

"I was just trying to be honest so you wouldn't risk embarrassing yourself."

Janet finally looked up, her eyes burning brightly. "Friends don't hurt each other's feelings, even for the sake of honesty. That's why I didn't say anything about those oatmeal cookies you baked for the book club meeting the other night."

"What about them?"

"Well, if you want me to be *honest*, they were so hard and dry that I was afraid someone might break a tooth."

Margaret blanched. "That's my grandmother's secret recipe, which just happens to be quite a favorite of Rev. Hale."

Abby's hope for spending a pleasant afternoon with two of her closest friends was quickly fading. She tried once more to change the subject.

"Speaking of Rev. Hale, I thought we might ask him to emcee the talent show. He has such a nice voice and I'm sure he'd do a wonderful job."

But neither Margaret nor Janet was listening to her, too caught up in their own hurt feelings.

Janet's eyes misted with tears. "I'm sorry I even brought up singing at the talent show."

"So am I," Margaret said, her mouth trembling. "You're blowing this all out of proportion."

Janet rose to her feet. "I don't think so." Then she turned to Abby. "I'm sorry, but I've lost my appetite."

And with that, Janet walked out of the restaurant. Abby watched her go in disbelief, bewildered by what had just happened. One moment they were all having a pleasant lunch together and the next moment their committee meeting was in shambles.

Margaret sniffed. "Well, I can't believe Janet made such a big scene over one little comment."

"Her feelings were hurt," Abby said gently, wanting to mend this rift between her friends before it grew any wider. "She thought you were insulting her singing ability."

Margaret stared at her. "That's not what I said at all!"

"I know," Abby replied, "but I think what got lost in all of this is that Janet wanted to sing something as a tribute to her mother and was hurt by your suggestion that it wasn't a good idea."

"Well, she insulted my grandmother's cookie recipe," Margaret retorted. "Maybe you think my oatmeal cookies are hard and dry too."

"Not at all," Abby assured her. "I had two of them at the last meeting."

"Then why are you taking Janet's side?"

"I'm not taking anybody's side," Abby explained. "I just think if you apologize to Janet, this whole thing will blow over."

"Apologize?" Tears welled in Margaret's eyes. "I already apologized. What about her apology to me? Obviously, you think I'm the one at fault here, Abby."

Margaret pushed her chair back from the table and rose to her feet. "I'm sorry if I ruined lunch for everyone. Maybe it's better if I just go home now. We can get together later to coordinate finding performers for the talent show."

"Margaret . . ." Abby began, but her friend turned on her heel and walked away.

Abby stared at the empty table, uncertain whether to follow Margaret or give her time to cool off. Obviously, neither of her friends was ready to forgive the other. Abby just hoped this squall between them would soon blow over.

"Hello, Abby."

She looked up to find Gary Diggs standing next to her chair. She'd been so caught up in the drama between Margaret and Janet that she hadn't seen him arrive at the restaurant.

"Hello," she replied, feeling a little flustered.

"Do you have a moment?"

"Of course," she said, hoping her afternoon could still be salvaged. Maybe he was going to tell her that his investigation of Hugo had fizzled and he'd discovered the real Howard Barnaby. "Please sit down."

Gary took the chair abandoned by Janet. "I promise not to keep you long. I know you're a busy woman."

That was an understatement, but she was too curious about what he had to say to hurry him along. "I'm taking a long lunch today."

He smiled. "Good. Then you won't mind if I ask you about the donations to the conservatory."

His remark confused her. "What about them?"

"How are they handled?" Gary asked. "Is Mr. Baron accountable to anyone for the contributions that come into the conservatory or does everyone just trust his figures?"

Abby tensed. "As the Curator, he's in charge of all financial matters of the conservatory. He does an excellent job, by the way. There have never been any financial improprieties connected to the conservatory."

"None that you're aware of, anyway," Gary said, then moved on before she could reply. "I've uncovered some additional information about Howard Barnaby. Indisputable facts that make me even more convinced that Hugo is Barnaby."

Abby now deeply regretted asking Gary to join her at the table. "I have a feeling you were convinced before you even arrived on Sparrow Island. Are you certain you're not cherry-picking these facts to fit your theory?"

He grinned, almost as if he enjoyed sparring with her. "Let me lay them out for you, Abby. Then you can decide for yourself."

Despite her distrust of him, Abby was ready to hear his evidence. Then maybe she could find a way to prove to him that he was all wrong about Hugo.

"Fact one," Gary began. "Hugo Baron's been visiting a widow by the name of Regina Downey in Seattle for the last three months."

Regina Downey. Abby remembered Wilma's remark that a Mrs. Downey kept calling the conservatory asking to talk to Hugo. Perhaps he was involved with the woman. That thought unsettled her. Especially the fact that he'd been keeping it a secret. Hugo had never struck her as the type of man to sneak around.

"So you've been following him?" Abby asked, wondering just how long Gary Diggs had been conducting this investigation.

"Let's just say I have my sources." Gary folded his hands on the table, the picture of confidence. "Do you even know who Regina Downey is?"

"No. Should I?"

He smiled. "Regina Downey was a famous actress in the forties and fifties. Only she went by the stage name of Regina Wilder then."

Abby realized she *had* heard of her, remembering all the glamour shots in the fashion magazines she and Mary used to buy as teenagers.

"Regina's a very wealthy woman now, just like all of

Barnaby's victims. Eight marriages to millionaires and subsequent divorces was a profitable sideline for her. However, I think this time Regina has met her match."

"Is that all?" Abby challenged. "You think because Hugo may be friends with this woman that makes him a con man? That's pretty flimsy evidence, Gary."

"Then how about this," he countered. "Hugo was born in the small town of Jasper, Maryland, but left home at the age of sixteen under mysterious circumstances.

"What kind of mysterious circumstances?"

Gary shrugged. "No one seems to know the entire story. I've just heard bits and pieces. Not quite enough, I'm afraid, to come to any conclusions. Did you even know he was from Maryland?"

Abby searched her memory. "I'm not sure if he ever mentioned it."

Gary smiled. "Strange, don't you think?"

His tone made her skin prickle. "I think that you're trying to manipulate these so-called facts to fit your theory," Abby said. "So far all that I've heard is that he's friends with a woman in the state of Washington and was born in Maryland."

Gary shook his head. "You seem to think I'm maliciously trying to destroy your boss. That's not it at all. I'm simply conducting an investigation—one that seems to keep leading me right to Hugo."

"We both know you've already made up your mind about him."

Gary held up his hands. "Hey, if you have any exculpatory evidence that proves Hugo Baron is not Howard Barnaby, I'll be happy to take a look at it."

Abby wished she could find a way to wipe that smug smile off of his face. Proving a negative was certainly more difficult than coming up with loosely based assertions that didn't prove anything.

"I'll give you the best evidence I have at the moment," she told him. "I know that Hugo Baron's not Howard Barnaby because I trust him. So do my parents and the congregation at Little Flock and the rest of his friends on Sparrow Island. Despite what you think, I believe I'm a good judge of character. If my word isn't good enough for you, then I don't know what else to say."

He got up from the table. "Thank you for giving me some of your time today, Abby. You may want to take a look into those conservatory donations, though, just to make certain your trust is not misplaced."

She had no intention of looking into the conservatory's financial records. That would be an insult to Hugo. She'd seen much too recently how insults could injure a friendship.

Abby was still fuming long after Gary Diggs left. He'd stopped by her table just to rattle her, passing along rumors about Hugo to make her doubt him.

She wished Gary had never come to Sparrow Island.

Even more, Abby wished she could brush off everything he'd just told her. But despite her protestations, Gary's so-called facts kept lingering.

Why didn't Hugo mention his relationship with Regina Downey to me? What makes Gary believe that Hugo left his hometown under mysterious circumstances?

Ida arrived at the table with another pitcher of iced tea. "How about a refill, Abby?"

"Oh yes, thank you."

Ida poured the tea, the ice clinking against the glass. "That guy sure does ask a lot of questions."

"You mean Gary?" Abby said, assuming Ida had seen him sitting at her table."

Ida nodded. "Is he doing a story on Hugo or something?"

"Not exactly." Abby took a drink of her iced tea, trying to gather her thoughts. "Why? What did Gary ask you?"

The waitress shrugged. "Nothing too specific. Just how long Hugo had lived here and if he ever talked about his past. Stuff like that."

Abby didn't like the idea of Gary interrogating Hugo's friends and acquaintances on Sparrow Island. But the only way to stop him was to find the real Howard Barnaby and Abby was no closer to doing that now than she had been a week ago.

"He seems pretty nice, though," Ida continued. "He even paid for your lunch."

"He did?" Abby asked in surprise.

"He sure did." Ida grinned. "So I guess you got a free lunch today."

A customer called out to Ida and she left Abby alone at the table. Her free lunch had left her with indigestion, thanks to Gary and the argument between two of her best friends. At least she now knew that Gary wasn't going to back off his investigation.

If Abby wanted to prove him wrong she had no time to waste.

CHAPTER 🌹 EIGHT

On SATURDAY MORNING, Abby arrived at the conservatory to check on her wildlife patients in the lab. She hadn't slept well the night before, troubled by the conflict between Margaret and Janet, as well as by her unexpected meeting with Gary Diggs. She'd prayed about it this morning, finding comfort in her Bible.

"I will send you rain in its season, and the ground will yield its crops and the trees of the field their fruit" (Leviticus 26:4).

Abby knew rain fell in every person's life, dampening their spirit but ultimately allowing them to grow. She needed to have faith in God's plan for herself and all of her friends and family.

When she reached the door to the lab, Abby unlocked it, then walked inside. The bright morning sun shone through the high windows, lighting the entire room. That's when she saw it.

An egg.

One perfect greenish-white egg in the nest Quackers had been building for the last week. Mallards liked to keep their nests well-hidden, usually in a deep depression in the ground or high aboveground in a tree joint. Abby had accommodated those instincts by altering the duck's cage to make room for a forked tree branch where Quackers could place her nest.

Then Abby had added grass and leaves to the cage every day, trying to simulate the natural materials the mother duck would find in the wild.

Quackers had done the rest, forming the materials into the shape of a bowl and lining it with downy soft feathers plucked from her breast.

The mother duck stood at the water bottle now, apparently unconcerned with Abby's presence. That was a good sign. Sometimes wildlife in captivity became so upset by the intrusion of a human that they accidentally injured their young.

Abby slowly approached the cage, ready to stop if Quackers became agitated. But the duck simply ignored her, sipping at the water, then dipping her beak into the feed trough.

Abby knelt down on the floor so that she presented even less of a threat. She was eye level with the nest now, able to see God's perfect creation nestled in the haven of leaves, grass and feathers that Quackers had gathered together.

The greenish egg was perfectly formed and would soon be followed by others. Mallards usually laid about eight to twelve eggs total, averaging one a day.

Her mind brightened as she thought about the ducklings cradled inside those eggs, just waiting to enter the world—ducklings that would soon become part of life on Sparrow Island.

Though she had observed countless nests with eggs or fledgling birds in them, Abby had never become jaded about the miracle of life. And it was especially poignant when the mother duck had to overcome both a broken wing and chocolate toxicity to bring her young into the world.

Abby added some grain to Quackers' trough and was refilling the water bottle when the door to the lab opened and Hugo stepped inside.

"Good morning," he said, looking informally dapper in a pair of khaki slacks and an olive green sports shirt.

Abby put her finger to her lips, then motioned him toward Quackers' cage. Hugo smiled when he saw the egg in the nest.

"Look at that," he breathed, moving beside Abby. "It's one of God's miracles, isn't it?"

Abby nodded, warmed by the fact that Hugo shared her awe. "Her eggs won't hatch for about a month, so that's going to delay releasing Quackers into the wild. We don't want to do anything to disturb the nest or put the ducklings at risk from predators."

"What kind of predators?"

"Foxes and raccoons," Abby explained. "Along with snapping turtles and even large fish when the ducklings are in the water. There's a fine art to releasing ducklings into the wild. You want to do it soon enough for them to adapt to their environment, but not until they're strong enough to survive on their own."

"But Quackers will protect them, too, won't she?" Hugo asked.

Abby nodded. "Female mallards are very protective of their young. She'll keep track of them and gather them up if they scatter. She'll also use certain behaviors to scare off potential predators, such as squawking or flapping her wings."

"Fascinating," Hugo murmured. He stepped closer to the cage for a better look. "I know it's probably selfish of me, but I'm glad we get to witness this."

"Not selfish at all," Abby assured him. "This is what spring is all about—the renewal of life."

Quackers began to flap her wings, signaling that she'd had enough company for one day. Abby and Hugo slowly withdrew.

"This is a lovely way to start the weekend," Hugo said.

Abby agreed. Hugo's passion for the wonders of nature matched her own. That was one of the reasons she'd let him talk her into moving back to Sparrow Island to work as the Associate Curator. He treasured all of God's handiwork just as she did. It seemed impossible to her that anyone could suspect he was a con man.

"Can you give me an update on the Rites of Spring exhibit?" Hugo asked her. "The opening's in six days."

Excitement rippled through Abby. "It's almost complete. The dioramas turned out well, and I think you'll be very impressed with the three-dimensional timeline of Sparrow Island's transition into spring."

He smiled. "You always impress me, Abby. I'm sure it will be a tremendous success."

"I'm planning to work on it this afternoon, if you'd like to join me. I'd like your opinion on a couple of the geological displays."

"I'm sorry, but I can't help you today." Regret flashed in his eyes. "I have other plans this afternoon."

She waited for him to explain, but Hugo remained silent, looking slightly uncomfortable. Heat washed over her cheeks when she realized he wasn't going to share his plans with her.

"No problem," she said hastily. "I can manage on my own."

"I'll be happy to take a look at the display on Monday," he told her. "Will that be soon enough?"

"Of course," she assured him, suddenly feeling a distance between them that unsettled her. Hugo wasn't a secretive person, but she sensed he was keeping something from her now.

Or maybe she was just paranoid because Gary Diggs had planted seeds of doubt in her mind.

Whatever the reason, she didn't want it to affect their friendship. That's why she needed to tell him about her encounter with Gary the day before. The fewer secrets between them, the better.

"I ran into that private investigator at the Springhouse Café yesterday."

Hugo arched a brow. "Oh?"

She took a deep breath. "I'm afraid he's still trying to prove that you're Howard Barnaby and . . ."

Despite her desire not to withhold information from him, Abby couldn't bring herself to mention Gary's insinuation about Regina Downey. Especially when she thought there might be some truth to it.

"And?" Hugo prompted.

"And he mentioned that you were born in Jasper, Maryland, but left there under mysterious circumstances when you were a teenager."

Hugo sighed, then turned toward the window. "I see."

Abby moved closer. "I don't care if it's true or not, Hugo. You don't owe me or Gary Diggs or anyone an explanation."

Hugo turned to face her. "Yet, if I say nothing, it only makes me look guilty, doesn't it? That's the conundrum I face in all of this, Abby. My silence is taken as guilt, but explanations look like excuses."

"Only to those people who don't know you."

Hugo pondered her words, then shrugged. "Perhaps. But you must be curious about his assertion. Who wouldn't be when Mr. Diggs throws out such a tantalizing phrase like *mysterious circumstances?*"

She couldn't deny it. That comment by Gary *had* piqued her interest. Abby knew so little about Hugo's early years, though now she wondered if there was good reason for it. Perhaps he'd had an unhappy childhood, something Abby had never experienced.

She knew she'd been greatly blessed in her life. Abby's childhood had been filled with laughter and learning. Growing up on the farm and on the sea, she'd been free to discover all the wonders of nature. Sometimes it was easy to forget that other people didn't have good memories of their youth.

Judging by the expression she now saw on Hugo's face, he must have been one of them.

"I know all that I need to know about you, Hugo," she said gently. "That you're a good man and a wonderful friend."

He smiled at her declaration, but shook his head. "No, I'm afraid that's not enough. Mr. Diggs has opened a Pandora's box, but I have no qualms about letting you peek inside, Abby. You, too, are a good woman and a wonderful friend."

She warmed at his words, wondering how she could ever doubt him. And yet, those nagging questions remained.

"Shall we step outside?" he suggested. "It's a beautiful day."

Abby followed him out of the building and into the warm spring sunshine. White clouds dotted the blue horizon and the song of a scarlet tanager serenaded them as they walked toward the creek.

The scent of freshly mowed grass clippings and the salty brine of the ocean perfumed the air. At this moment, she could think of nowhere else on earth she would rather be.

Looking into Hugo's face, Abby could see that he was somewhere else right now. Somewhere in the past. She waited, wanting to let him speak in his own time. The gurgle of the water flowing over the rocks filled the silence between them.

"My mother died when I was eleven years old," Hugo began at last. "She'd been ill for several years, but despite her frailty she was the foundation of our small family."

Abby's heart ached for him. She couldn't imagine losing a parent at such a young and vulnerable age.

"We were all lost without her," Hugo said, his voice tight. "Especially my father. He remarried less than a year later to a woman who was nothing like my mother. He was simply looking for someone to save him."

Hugo's gaze fixed on the flowing water. "You see, his faith was built on shifting sand."

His words reminded her of the scripture from the Book of Matthew.

"Therefore everyone who hears these words of mine and puts them into practice is like a wise man who built his house on the rock. The rain came down, the streams rose and the winds blew and beat against the house; yet it did not fall, because it had its foundation on the rock" (Matthew 7:24–27).

"My stepmother wasn't a bad woman," he explained. "Eva brought three sons with her into the marriage, two boys older than me and one younger. She worked hard to be a good mother, but she always wanted more. More money, more furniture for the house, more clothes. Her sons were just like her."

He met Abby's gaze. "When I was sixteen her oldest son accused me of stealing money from his room. I denied it, but my father didn't believe me."

She saw the pain in his eyes and tried to imagine the anguish of his father's betrayal.

"That's when I left home and never returned," Hugo said softly. "No doubt my stepbrothers told people in town I'd left after stealing money. That must be the mysterious circumstance that Gary Diggs referred to, although I'm amazed anyone in Jasper would even remember me after all of these years."

Abby didn't know what to say to him. She was sorry she had made Hugo relive such a painful memory. "It must have been very difficult for you to leave home at such a young age."

He gave her a wistful smile. "Difficult, yes, but it led me on a path that I'll never regret. I truly learned the meaning of faith, Abby. When I left home I had no money, no food, and only the clothes on my back. But I did have God and no one could ever take Him away from me."

She could hear the conviction in his voice and see the joy shining in his eyes.

"I felt His presence in my life then," he continued, "and I knew I could always count on His guidance and protection."

Her eyes misted at his words and she knew Hugo's faith was built upon the rock. His story only made her more determined to find the real Howard Barnaby so that no one else ever questioned his integrity.

A robin landed in the shallow part of the creek and began washing its wings. Hugo chuckled at the sight, then turned to

Abby. "It all happened so many years ago. I've long since for-given my father. I know that he loved me in his own way."

Abby knew that forgiveness was the only path to peace. She was glad Hugo had opened his heart to his father, despite his pain.

"I'm honored that you trusted me enough to tell me, Hugo," Abby said softly. "I'm sure both of your parents would be very proud of you."

He smiled. "Thank you for being such a good listener." Then he looked up at the sky. "Looks like it might rain soon."

Abby loved a spring rain, especially the earthy smell of the air the next morning. "So it does. I'd better finish gathering the moss for the—"

"Oh, look at the time," Hugo interjected, scowling at his watch. "I'm sorry, Abby. I need to go."

She watched him hurry off, perplexed by his sudden depar-ture. He hadn't even let her finish her sentence. Hugo jogged to his car in the parking lot, then pulled out, his tires squeal-ing on the surface.

In all the time she'd worked at the conservatory, she'd never seen Hugo in such a rush. It was completely out of character.

She watched his car until it was just a speck in the distance. Then she turned back to the creek. Hugo had shared a difficult part of his life with her, then he'd run off.

What does it mean?

By the time she arrived home that afternoon, Abby still hadn't figured it out. She walked into the house, unloading her bag onto the kitchen counter and admonishing herself to unload her worries as well.

She had the rest of the weekend to come up with a plan to search for Howard Barnaby. Once she found him, all her doubts about Hugo would vanish. Then she could focus her attention on the Rites of Spring exhibit and the upcoming talent show.

Abby looked out the window and saw Mary on the deck. Her sister sat by the patio table, her arms up to her elbows in dirt as she repotted a plant. Finnegan sat dutifully beside her, a smudge of the potting soil on his nose.

Smiling to herself, Abby poured two glasses of lemonade. Though gray clouds still filled the sky, it hadn't rained yet and she wanted to take advantage of the dry weather to enjoy the rest of her Saturday.

"Hello there," Abby said as she stepped out onto the deck. "You look like you're ready for a break. How about a glass of lemonade?"

Mary looked up from her wheelchair, then brushed the dirt from her hands. "Thanks, I could use it."

Something in her sister's voice didn't sound right. Abby handed a glass to her sister, then sat down in the white rocking chair. "Are you okay?"

Mary took a deep drink of her lemonade. Then she lowered her glass with a long sigh. "Oh, Abby."

She could hear the quaver in her sister's voice and tension coiled within her. "Mary, what is it?"

"Janet just called me. She resigned as codirector of the talent show and as the president of the book club."

"Oh no," Abby gasped, stunned that it had come to this.

"Oh yes," Mary countered. "I tried to talk her out of it, but she was adamant. I've never heard her so upset."

Abby had hoped Janet and Margaret had made amends by now. Obviously, that hadn't happened.

"I can't believe she'd just quit," Abby said. "That book club means too much to her."

"I know." Mary shook her head. "While we were talking on the phone, she kept bringing up things from the past that Margaret had said or done that she now sees as slights against her."

The breeze caressed Abby's face as she sat on the deck. The rift between Janet and Margaret affected everyone around them, like the ripples created from throwing a stone in a pond.

"Does Margaret know Janet resigned?" Abby asked, hoping it might provoke her into trying to make amends.

"Yes," Mary replied. "I called all the book club members to let them know. Margaret thinks Janet is just overreacting and that this will all blow over." A smile haunted her lips. "Then she asked me if I thought her oatmeal cookies were hard and dry at the last meeting."

Finnegan yawned, his teeth gleaming in the sunlight. Then he lay down on the deck, his eyes drooping.

"I'm feeling a little tired, myself," Mary said, leaning over to pet the dog's head. "Shall we go inside?"

Finnegan blinked, then lumbered to his feet as Mary swept loose dirt from the table.

"Do you need any help?" Abby asked her, watching her sister tidy up.

"Could you grab my watch?" Mary asked her. "It's on the storage chest."

Abby got up and walked over to it. "Where?"

"Right on top."

But it wasn't there. Abby looked on the floor of the deck, but there was no sign of the watch there either. "It's not here."

"It has to be," Mary said, rolling the wheelchair over to her. "I put it right . . ."

Her words trailed off as she stared at the empty top of the storage chest. "I took it off when I started repotting the plants."

"You're sure you put it on the storage chest?"

"Positive," Mary said. "I went inside for a quick lunch, then came right back out. It has to be here somewhere."

But it wasn't. They looked all over the deck and even underneath it.

Abby could see the disappointment in her sister's eyes. Henry had given Mary the unique gold and pearl watch as a Christmas gift.

"What do you think happened to it?" Abby asked her.

"I have no idea." Mary paled as she looked at her sister. "Is it possible the thief took it?"

That thought had already occurred to Abby, as implausible as it seemed. Surely there had to be some other explanation. "I guess it's possible."

"But not probable," Mary said, then she sighed. "I guess we have another mystery on our hands."

CHAPTER ❧ NINE

THE TWO SISTERS SPENT another twenty minutes searching for the watch. They retraced Mary's path from the deck to the kitchen and back again, but there was no sign of her watch anywhere.

"It has to be here," Mary muttered, looking around the deck once more. "The longer we look, the more I think it was stolen."

"But would someone sneak up on our deck in broad daylight to steal a watch?"

Mary shrugged. "I wish I could think of some other explanation."

"You said yourself that you were only inside for a short time to eat lunch. How could a thief pick that exact moment to walk up on our deck and steal your watch? How would he even know it was there?"

Mary spun her wheelchair around and headed for the house. "I don't know, but it's a reasonable conclusion considering all the other thefts that have been happening here lately."

Abby knew she was right. Ellen Stanton had told her as much the night of Hugo's dinner party. A petty thief was roaming the island, stealing small items both day and night. Yet, Abby didn't like to think of some intruder coming that close to their home.

"I don't know what to think," Mary said, the dog walking beside her as she rolled her wheelchair through the sliding glass doors and into the living room. "Surely Finnegan would have barked if someone had been out on the deck."

Abby nodded, but the missing watch still bothered her. If, indeed, there was a thief on the island he . . . or she . . . was stealing not only their possessions but their sense of security.

"I probably did misplace it," Mary said, uncertainty clouding her eyes. "I am getting older. My memory probably isn't as good as it used to be."

"Nonsense," Abby replied, sorry now that she'd questioned Mary's belief that her watch had been stolen. Her sister wasn't paranoid and she certainly wasn't experiencing memory problems.

Abby had simply not wanted to admit that a criminal could come that close to them. Instead of facing her fear, she'd chosen denial and probably hurt her sister's feelings in the process.

"I'm sorry I doubted you," Abby said, sliding the door closed behind them. "If you said you put the watch on the storage chest, then somebody must have taken it. I think you should call Henry and make a report."

Mary hesitated a moment, then nodded. "I think I'll do that."

She moved toward the phone as Abby headed toward the kitchen.

"Hey, Abby?" her sister called out to her.

Abby stepped back into the living room. "Yes?"

"I forgot to tell you that a letter arrived for you today. It's on the counter."

"Thanks." Abby walked into the kitchen and picked up the small stack of mail next to the microwave. She sorted through some flyers and advertisements before coming upon a small parchment envelope with her name and address inscribed on the front in beautiful calligraphy.

Curious, Abby reached for the letter opener and slit open the seal. Then she pulled out the card, also written in calligraphy.

Dear Dr. Stanton,

We request the pleasure of your company on Thursday, March 22, at two o'clock for afternoon tea. Formal dress is not required. We look forward to meeting you.

Paul & Anne Riley

Abby turned the card over and saw the Rileys address and phone number embossed in gold. She'd never met the Rileys before and was intrigued by the invitation. Perhaps all the book club members had received one.

Mary rolled into the kitchen. "Henry's going to make a police report when he comes over to watch a movie with me this evening," she told Abby. "He's received more calls about stolen items this week."

"Then I'm glad you talked to him about it," Abby replied. She held up her invitation. "Did you get one of these?"

"No." Mary moved closer to her. "What is it?"

"An invitation to tea from the Rileys." She handed it to Mary so she could read it.

"The wording's very formal," Mary observed. "Almost like they're royalty. I've heard they're a little eccentric."

"Have you ever met them?"

Mary shook her head. "Paul Riley has called to order flowers for his wife before, but he always sends his butler to pick them up."

"They have a butler?"

Mary laughed. "Well, that's what they call him. I have to admit he has the demeanor of a butler. He seems very stern and proper."

Abby took the invitation from her and studied it again. "I wonder why they want to see me."

"Maybe they're interested in donating to the conservatory," Mary ventured. "I believe all the books they've written have made them quite wealthy. Just look at their generous gift of the library wing."

Abby supposed she was right, but assumed they'd contact Hugo about a potential donation. Then another thought hit her.

What if they'd heard the rumors about Hugo and didn't trust him?

That possibility made her heart sink. She sincerely hoped that wasn't the reason for the Rileys' invitation.

"So are you going?" Mary asked her.

"I wouldn't miss it," Abby declared, mentally reviewing her calendar. Thursday afternoon was clear, so there weren't any time conflicts. All she'd be doing was putting the finishing touches on the display in preparation for the exhibit opening on Friday evening.

"If you don't mind, I think I'll go clean up," Mary said, heading toward her room. "Then I may take a short nap."

"Okay." Abby placed the invitation in her bag. "Remind

Henry that the opening is black tie so he doesn't forget to order his tux."

Mary grinned. "It's already done. I'm not about to miss out on an occasion to dress up. Do you know what you're wearing yet?"

Abby thought about it for a moment. "Probably the same outfit I wore to the Wonderful World of Wings exhibit."

Mary shook her head. "You deserve a new dress after all the work you've done on this display. Let's go shopping this week and find something spectacular for you to wear."

Abby nodded, knowing it was futile to argue with her sister. Besides, with Mary along, Abby would be able to find something flattering but still affordable.

After Mary retreated to her bedroom, Abby headed upstairs to do some research on her computer. She sat down at the desk, placing her glass of lemonade on a sandstone coaster. Then she typed the name Regina Downey into the search engine.

Almost immediately dozens of links began to appear on the screen. Abby clicked on the top one, then read the online news article from *The Boston Globe.*

Regina Downey, the former 1950s screen siren known as Regina Wilder and now the widow of the late Maximus Downey, is stepping down as the executive director of the multimillion dollar Downey Foundation.

During her tenure, Mrs. Downey directed funds to several educational institutions in the Boston area and sponsored thousands of scholarships for at-risk youth. Her sudden departure came as a surprise to the board of directors.

Abby read the article a second time, trying to glean more information from the short piece. Then she clicked on a few other links, but most of them just listed the many charitable organizations that the Downey Foundation had helped and Mrs. Downey's role at the foundation.

One of the links, however, included a color photograph of Regina Downey along with information that she was relocating to the state of Washington.

That was three months ago.

Abby stared at the photograph. Regina Downey was still a striking woman with snow white hair and a demure smile. No reason was given for her move across the country or why she'd retired from her late husband's influential foundation.

Abby knew what Gary Diggs would say—that Hugo had romanced Regina into giving up everything for him. That she'd left her home and her job to be close to him. That Hugo must have known her before she'd moved to Washington. How else could their relationship have developed in such a short amount of time?

She couldn't deny that some of those assertions seemed plausible. Hugo had never mentioned Regina Downey to her, yet he was making unexpected trips to the mainland. And the woman kept in constant contact with him.

And she was very, very rich.

Abby sighed as she turned off the computer. It was all speculation at this point, yet she couldn't bring herself to ask Hugo about it. Part of her was afraid that he'd take offense at her questions.

The other part of her worried that maybe she wouldn't like his answers.

So she needed to go in a different direction.

Abby pulled out her list of possible Howard Barnabys and placed them in alphabetical order. It consisted of single men living on Sparrow Island who fit the profile given to her by Gary Diggs.

She'd eliminated several already just by cross-referencing to archived copies of the Sparrow Island newspaper with the month that Howard had spent with Vanessa. Any articles that mentioned one of Abby's suspects by name made it easy to cross him off the list. Even Howard Barnaby couldn't be in two places at the same time.

She was happy to exclude Rick DeBow and William Jansen and several others of her friends and neighbors. The juggler, Mr. Danker, had been excluded when Abby met his wife at The Green Grocer. They'd been happily married for forty years and had traveled with the circus together.

Unfortunately, she hadn't been able to exclude Hugo. And she was no closer to identifying the real Howard Barnaby.

Abby heard the shower running in the bathroom below her, then let her gaze drift over the impossibly long list once more. It was no use. Despite her best effort, she was no closer to solving this case.

It was time to admit to herself that she might never find Howard Barnaby.

ON MONDAY EVENING, the Sparrow Island Book Club held a special meeting at the library to discuss the fundraiser. Abby had been hoping that Janet would change her mind about her resignation, but she was noticeably absent from their group.

William cleared his throat. "As the vice president of the book club, I guess I'll run tonight's meeting."

"Is it true, then?" Naomi asked. "Did Janet really resign?"

Margaret shifted her weight on the chair beside Abby. "She'll be back."

"But what happened?" Sandy looked around the group. "Is she having personal problems or a problem with our book club?"

Margaret pressed her mouth together, but didn't say anything. So Abby tried to find a way to tactfully broach the subject. "The talent committee had a meeting last Friday and I'm afraid Janet took offense to part of the conversation. The next day, she called Mary and told her she was resigning both as the codirector of the talent show and the president of our group."

An uncomfortable silence followed her explanation and Abby knew everyone wanted to know exactly what had happened. But it wasn't her place to discuss the conversation between Margaret and Janet, especially when it would be impossible to repeat it word-for-word or for anyone to understand all the emotions involved.

The last thing Abby wanted was for the book club members to start taking sides in this situation.

"The good news is that the Community Center has agreed to let us hold the talent show for no rental cost," William said. "However, in light of these new circumstances we need to decide if we want to continue with our fundraiser."

"I don't know," Sandy said. "It just won't be the same without Janet."

"I agree," Edmonia chimed in. "Now we're down to seven members. This talent show's going to be a big production and take up a lot of our time. What if we lose more members in the meantime?"

"That's not going to happen," Margaret assured her. "I'm

sure this will all blow over and Janet will be back here next week to preside over the meeting."

Abby wasn't so sure. She also couldn't understand Margaret's refusal to take responsibility for her part in the incident. She might not have meant to insult Janet, but she'd hurt her friend's feelings. Both of them were too stubborn to make the first move.

But were they stubborn enough to lose their friendship over it?

William looked around the group. "Is that the consensus, then? Do we cancel the fundraiser?"

"I don't want to cancel it," Margaret said. "I realize it might mean more work with just the seven of us running the show, but I still want to find a way to donate to the library."

Naomi nodded her agreement. "I've already been telling patrons about it and informed the Rileys of our plans. If we back out now, it might look like we're not supporting the library expansion."

"I agree," Mary said. "We've made a commitment to helping the library. I'm willing to handle the director duties on my own and we've already divided into our committees."

Abby knew her sister wasn't a quitter. It wouldn't be easy for Mary to direct the talent show by herself, but if anybody could do it, her big sister could.

"Shall we vote on it?" William asked the group. "All those who are in favor of continuing with the talent show, raise your hand."

Seven hands rose in the air, much to Abby's relief. The book club was such a small and intimate group that she'd been afraid Janet's departure might tear them apart. She was happy to see that they were willing to stick together and carry on with the talent show. With any luck, Janet would be rejoining them again soon.

"Then it looks like it's a go," William said with a smile. "The talent show's only twelve days away, so why don't we grab some refreshments, then meet with our committees. Hopefully, we'll have some time left to discuss *Hawaii* since we didn't get to it last week."

Abby stood up, aware that Margaret had an eagle eye on the refreshment table. She'd brought her oatmeal cookies again, no doubt to prove to herself that everyone enjoyed them. Abby intended to help herself to two cookies just to keep the peace in the group.

After helping themselves to some cookies and tea, Abby and Margaret huddled together to discuss the progress of their talent hunt.

"I've received two phone calls already," Margaret said, "and the ad hasn't even come out in the newspaper yet."

"Really?" Abby said, nibbling on a cookie. "Who called?"

"Warren Meyers and Frank Holloway."

Both names surprised her. Warren owned a whale watching tour boat called the *Sea Star* and was raising a seventeen-year-old daughter on his own. Frank owned the hardware store and was the last person she'd expect to perform onstage.

"The Meyers are going to perform a dance routine," Margaret explained. "Warren sounded very excited about it and somewhat surprised that Mercedes had agreed to do it with him."

"And Frank?"

"He didn't sound excited on the phone, but then he never

does," Margaret said as she watched Abby take another bite of her cookie.

They were chewy and moist, definitely better than last week's batch, though she'd had no complaints then either.

"They're good, aren't they?" Margaret asked.

Abby nodded. "Very good."

"I realized that I didn't put in enough brown sugar the last time. That's why they weren't as good as usual."

A simple mistake. Yet, why couldn't Margaret see that Janet's feelings had been bruised by a careless comment about her singing just as Margaret's had been about her baking?

"So what talent does Frank want to perform?" Abby asked her.

Margaret shrugged her shoulders. "He was so gruff on the phone, I didn't have a chance to ask him. Would you mind stopping by his store to ask him?"

"Of course not," Abby replied.

Margaret's job as the school secretary made it difficult for her to get away during the day. Abby had flexibility in her schedule. Besides, she needed to pick up some supplies at the hardware store for the Rites of Spring exhibit.

"Someone contacted me too," Abby said. "Do you know Mrs. Mulligan?"

"Father Tim's housekeeper?"

Abby nodded. "She wants to perform an Irish step dance."

"Perfect," Margaret said. "Let's add her to the list." Then she glanced over at the refreshment table. "Looks like my cookie plate is almost empty. I'd better go refill it."

They parted company, Abby heading to the wastebasket to dispose of her paper plate and napkin.

"Isn't it a beautiful evening?" Edmonia said behind her.

Abby dumped her trash, then turned to face her hairdresser. The woman was glowing. Though usually cheerful, there was something different about Edmonia this evening.

"It certainly is," Abby replied. "Although, that seems to be the norm for Sparrow Island. I didn't realize how much I missed the wonderful climate until I came back home."

Edmonia dropped her paper plate into the trash. "Just think, after the new library wing is added we can hold our book club meetings in the courtyard on a lovely evening like this. Won't that be nice?"

Abby nodded, knowing that everyone in the community would enjoy the new addition. Perhaps that was the reason for Edmonia's beaming smile.

"By the way," Abby said, "I'd really like to get a trim before the opening of the new exhibit. Do you have any openings tomorrow?"

"Oh, I'm sorry, Abby," Edmonia said, though her grin belied her apology, "but I won't be in the shop tomorrow at all. I have a date!"

So that explained Edmonia's giddy mood. "A date?"

Edmonia moved closer to Abby and lowered her voice. "Oh, you should see him! He's *so* handsome. We met last week when he came into my shop for a haircut. He's got the most gorgeous thick white hair."

Abby smiled at her excitement. "Is he a tourist?"

"Oh, goodness no," Edmonia replied. "His name is Roman Dietz and he moved to Sparrow Island a year ago. He's quite a bit older than I am, but *so* distinguished. He makes me feel like a princess. He's taking me on a romantic picnic tomorrow on Orcas Island."

"He sounds wonderful."

"He is," Edmonia said dreamily. "The best part about it is that he's a former businessman, so he's interested in hearing all about the Silver Scissors. He even promised to give me some investment advice."

Alarms sounded in Abby's head. Edmonia's new boyfriend was older, distinguished and very interested in her business. Had she finally stumbled upon a real lead? If so, Edmonia was much younger than Barnaby's usual victims.

"I'd like to meet him sometime," Abby said, hoping her friend wasn't rushing into anything. Then again, Gary had described Howard Barnaby as irresistible.

"You will," she promised. "Roman and I have been spending so much time together. It's like we've known each other forever."

When Abby took her seat, the *Hawaii* discussion was already underway. They talked about the span of history in the book, as well as the rich tapestry of characters.

"The missionaries fascinated me," Sandy said. "The way they left their homes and families behind to travel to a strange new land."

"I thought the part about the leprosy colony was so interesting," Naomi commented, then she shivered, "and so chilling. Can you imagine the fear and hopelessness of living that way?"

"The formation of the islands at the beginning of the book was really boring to me," Mary said. "I wanted to read about the characters right away, so it put a damper on the experience for me. I should have just skipped over that chapter."

Abby loved participating in the book discussion, always eager to hear the different opinions. "Chapter one was a little dry," she agreed, "but the other chapters made up for it, especially the story about the Chinese immigrant Nyuk Tsin.

I thought her character was a wonderful example of the power of the human spirit."

"She certainly was a heroine in the story," William agreed, then looked around the group. "Any opinion on who best fit the role of a villain?"

While the book club members opined on his question, Abby thought about the real life villain on Sparrow Island. The identity of Howard Barnaby still eluded her. Just like the book they'd read, her search for the con man involved many twists and turns.

"What do you think, Abby?" William asked her as the book discussion began to wind down. "Is *Hawaii* a book you'd recommend to others?"

"Definitely," Abby replied without hesitation. "As I said before, the first chapter's a little dry, but if you stay the course you'll be richly rewarded."

That's what she intended to do with her investigation too. Stay the course. It was the only way she could prove that Hugo Baron was an innocent man.

CHAPTER ❧ TEN

THE NEXT DAY, ABBY entered Holloway's Hardware and saw Aaron, Frank Holloway's grandson, standing behind the counter.

At twenty-five, Aaron was tall and lanky, the opposite of his short, stocky grandfather. A smart young man, he'd drifted aimlessly for a while in a variety of jobs before finally taking a position at his grandfather's store.

"Hello, Dr. Stanton," Aaron said as he vigorously wiped off the counter with a dust rag. "How are you doing today?"

"I'm just fine," she replied, seeing no sign of Frank. "Is your grandfather here?"

"He stepped out for a minute," Aaron replied. "We're out of coffee, so he ran down to The Green Grocer to get some more. But maybe I can help you."

When Aaron had started working at the hardware store, he'd been clueless about tools and home repairs and construction. Some customers had even bypassed him in favor of his more knowledgeable grandfather. But he was a quick learner and had supplemented his on-the-job experience with books from the library.

"I need something to hang a wooden display board." Abby held out her arms. "It's about this wide and one-half inch thick. I want to suspend it from the ceiling."

Aaron brushed back his shaggy brown hair. "You could use eye screws and a wire. Do you know how heavy the board is?"

Abby considered the question. "It's fairly light. I can pick it up and carry it myself, if that helps to answer your question."

He walked around the counter and led her down one of the aisles. "Six eye screws ought to do the job," Aaron said. "And I'd recommend the ten gauge wire just to be on the safe side."

Aaron picked out the items for Abby, then they headed back to the front counter. "Will this be cash or charge today?"

"Go ahead and charge it to the conservatory, please," she replied.

As Aaron rang up the order, the door to the store opened and Frank walked inside cradling a can of coffee in the crook of his arm.

"Six dollars," he grumbled. "Can you believe it? A body can't even afford to drink coffee anymore the way the price has gone up. I remember when coffee only cost a few cents."

"Hello, Frank," Abby said, taking the sack Aaron handed her. "I was hoping I'd get a chance to speak with you."

Frank set the coffee can on the counter. "Can I help you with something, Abby?"

"Aaron's already taken very good care of me."

Pride shone in Frank's gray eyes. "Glad to hear it. He's been a big help around here. So why'd you want to see me, Abby?"

"Well, I heard you want to perform in the talent show."

He gaped at her. "What?"

"Hey, you could play the saw," Aaron exclaimed, then turned to Abby. "He can play a mean version of *Row, Row, Row Your Boat* on the saw. Business got kind of slow here the other day, and Grandad played an entire repertoire of songs."

Frank scowled at his grandson. "That doesn't mean I'm going to make a crazy fool of myself in front of the whole town."

"Would you rather perform some other talent?" Abby asked him. "Margaret gave me your name as a volunteer performer."

Frank sighed. "Then Margaret got my message all wrong. I didn't call to volunteer to perform in the talent show. I called to donate some brick pavers for the new courtyard at the library."

"Oh," Abby replied, surprised and pleased at the same time. "That's wonderful."

"Play the saw," Frank mumbled, casting an exasperated look at his grandson. "Of all the ridiculous ideas I ever heard."

Aaron shrugged. "Hey, it's for a good cause."

Another customer entered the store and Aaron hurried over to help him.

Frank turned back to Abby. "So, just let me know how many pavers you need and I'll order them."

"That's very generous of you."

He shrugged off her compliment. "I figure that library has saved me money in the long run. You should see the stack of books Aaron brings home every week so he can learn more about the hardware business."

Despite his gruff demeanor, Abby knew Frank Holloway had a soft heart. She also couldn't resist teasing him a little. "Are you sure you don't want to play the saw? We could have a sing along."

Frank chuckled. "Believe me, Abby, I'm not the kind of talent you want for that show. People might demand their money back."

She sensed Frank was being modest, but didn't argue with him. "I suppose I should get back to the conservatory. Thanks again, Frank."

Aaron gave her a wave as she headed out the door.

As Abby stepped onto the sheltered porch she saw the usual group of men who gathered there to swap stories. They drank Frank's expensive coffee and told tales from years past that seemed as real as if they had happened yesterday.

Only today's tale was all too recent.

"Ya seen that private investigator fella asking questions about Hugo Baron?" Abby heard one of the men say to his friends. "Sounds like there's something fishy going on with that guy."

Another man shook his head. "You just never know who to trust these days."

Her stomach lurched. Rumors about Hugo were already spreading through the community. Abby stepped toward them, hating to intrude but unable to just walk away.

"Good morning, gentlemen."

The men nodded their greeting.

"How ya doin, Abby?" asked Nub Higgins, a member of Little Flock.

Abby had known Nub since she was a young girl, though she'd never learned his real name. She could still remember when he had played the part of Moses in their Vacation Bible School skit, his deep voice leaving all the children awestruck. Only now the long gray beard he wore was real instead of fake.

"I'm just fine, Nub," she replied. "But I couldn't help

overhearing your conversation about Hugo. Do you mind telling me exactly what Gary Diggs is saying about him?"

"Gary Diggs?" Nub replied. "Is that the fellow's name?"

She nodded. "Yes. I'm afraid Gary's under the mistaken impression that Hugo is the man he's been searching for."

The men exchanged glances, then looked at Abby. "The thing is," Nub told, "nobody really knows much about Hugo's background. That's what this Diggs fellow has been asking all of us about. And we don't have the answers."

She understood their position. Abby herself had some questions about the holes in Hugo's past. She just didn't want those questions to turn into accusations without any proof.

"I'm sure the truth will come out soon," she told them. "In the meantime, I hope you'll give Hugo the benefit of the doubt. He's a good man."

Nub nodded. "We'll take your word for it, Abby. We know we can trust you."

"Thanks," she replied, wishing they'd trust in Hugo as well. He'd done so much for the conservatory and for Sparrow Island. "Have a nice day, gentlemen."

They wished her the same, then Abby got into her car and headed for the conservatory. Along the way, she thought some more about the conversation she'd heard on the porch and her spirits sank.

If Gary Diggs was casting aspersions about Hugo to everyone he met, how could she possibly prove him wrong without concrete proof of some kind?

She'd narrowed down her suspect list, but Abby still wasn't ready to name the con man. And she wasn't about to engage in Gary's tactics of smearing an innocent man.

But what if Hugo isn't innocent?

That thought came unbidden into her mind. She tried to ignore it, but Abby couldn't deny that Hugo acknowledged an acquaintance with Vanessa Ellsworth, as well as the fact that the woman had sent money to him. The time period of her meeting Howard Barnaby fit too.

A headache began to throb in her temple. The rumors around Hugo affected not only him but the conservatory as well. There would be a shadow of suspicion hanging over the opening of their Rites of Spring exhibit.

It wasn't fair and it wasn't right, but Abby didn't know how to stop it.

She also didn't want to tell Hugo that the situation was getting worse. He'd been so preoccupied lately that she didn't want to burden him further. Besides, Abby had promised to track down the real Howard Barnaby and so far she'd come up empty.

Abby pulled into the parking lot of the conservatory, but instead of heading for her office, she walked over to the observation platform and climbed to the top. The view from there always inspired her.

She walked to the rail, inhaling a deep breath of the crisp morning air. She could feel the tension ease from her shoulders as her gaze scanned the tree line to the edge of the water and beyond. It was a glorious reminder that God was watching over everything and that worrying was simply wasted energy.

"Who of you by worrying can add a single hour to his life?" (Matthew 6:27)

Abby sighed, realizing how often she needed to remember that Bible verse. It was very difficult not to worry—not to believe that she could control everything around her. But God was the only One in control. Abby needed to remember that and lean on Him for guidance in times of trouble.

She bowed her head, the sweet song of a meadowlark heralding forth as she began to pray aloud.

"Heavenly Father, take this worry from my heart and show me the path to the truth. Let me be a good friend to others, and most of all, help me to find a way to heal the rifts in my community. Amen."

By the time Abby descended the observation platform, her spirit felt renewed. She had a new bounce in her step as she made her way to the laboratory to check on Quackers.

The mallard sat contentedly on her nest, which now held four eggs. Both she and Quackers would have to be patient. The nest couldn't be moved, not without seriously risking the possibility that Quackers would abandon it. At least the duck seemed to be taking her prolonged captivity in stride.

Abby jotted down some notes about each of her wildlife patients, then quietly left the lab. As she walked out the door, she bumped into Bobby.

"Whoa," she said, reaching out a hand to balance them both. "What are you doing here?"

He grinned, adjusting the backpack slung over his shoulder. "We've got a late start at school today, so I thought I'd see how Quackers and her eggs are doing. How many does she have now?"

"Four," Abby told him. "It's hard to wait for them to hatch, isn't it?"

He nodded. "Very hard. But I've been practicing my juggling, so that makes the time go faster."

"How's it coming along?"

He grinned. "Do you want to see a demonstration?"

"I sure do."

Bobby pulled off his backpack as they entered the museum's back door, then reached inside for three yellow tennis balls. "I used to practice with apricots, but they got kind of squishy and started bursting when I dropped them." Bobby shook his head. "Do you know how hard it is to clean apricot stains off of a white shirt?"

Abby suppressed a smile. "I can imagine."

"Okay," Bobby said, placing two balls in one hand and one ball in the other. "Here I go."

Abby stepped back to give him some room as he tossed the first two tennis balls into the air. She watched in amazement as he began juggling all three of them in perfect unison.

"That's wonderful, Bobby," she said, impressed with how quickly he'd acquired the skill.

"Thanks," he replied. "I've been trying to learn how to toss one of them behind my back. Here goes . . ."

He pitched one of the balls high into the air above his head, then reached behind him to catch it. The ball glanced off his thumb and bounced onto the tile floor several times before finally landing in a plastic bucket down the hallway.

"Oops," Bobby said, catching the other two balls. "I guess I need to work on that some more."

"You've almost got it." Abby walked down the hallway to retrieve the errant tennis ball. When she reached the bucket, she saw cleaning supplies inside and assumed they belonged to Wallace, the new caretaker.

She'd only seen him a few times, usually when he was sweeping the hallway or dusting the offices. He seemed like a nice enough man and was very chatty. Sometimes it seemed that he'd rather talk than work.

In his late forties, Wallace was too young to fit her Howard

Barnaby profile. Otherwise, he'd probably be on her list of suspects.

When Abby removed the tennis ball from the bucket, she saw something unusual inside of it.

"Look at this," she murmured, pulling out a large gold coin with strange symbols on it. "It's just like the one you found in that empty cage in the lab."

"It's another Burmese coin." Bobby's eyes widened as he took the coin from Abby. "I sent a picutre of the first one to a coin collector I contacted online. She e-mailed me yesterday and identified it."

"Burmese?"

"A rare coin from Burma," Bobby explained. "They stopped making them a long time ago."

Once again, Bobby's intelligence and resourcefulness impressed her.

"So how did it get in Wallace's bucket?" Abby said, more to herself than to Bobby.

The boy shrugged, then dug the first coin out of his pocket and handed them both back to her. "I guess you could ask him." Then he glanced at his watch. "Uh-oh, I'd better get going."

She tossed him his tennis ball, then watched him place all three items in his backpack. "Have a good day at school."

"I will," he promised. He gave her a wave as he trotted out of the building to meet his mother who had been waiting for him.

Abby stayed there for a moment looking at the coin in her hand, then at the bucket. This coin was as much a mystery as the first one.

It also could be a clue in her search for Howard Barnaby.

If Bobby was right about the origin of these coins, then they could prove a connection to Vanessa Ellsworth, since Hugo had mentioned that Vanessa had lived in Burma when she was a child.

It made sense that Howard Barnaby would see the value in these rare coins. What didn't make sense was how one had ended up in a cage in her laboratory and the other had found its way into Wallace's bucket.

Bobby was right. She'd have to ask him.

BY LATE AFTERNOON, Abby was putting the finishing touches on the Rites of Spring timeline exhibit. She stood back, admiring her work and trying to evaluate if there was anything that she was missing.

"It looks wonderful," Wilma exclaimed, stepping into the workroom. "I especially like that the timeline shows how everything on the island changes in the spring."

"Thank you," Abby replied, feeling quite pleased with it herself. This display had taken a lot of time, but she'd learned a lot along the way and hoped that others would too.

"Have you seen Wallace?" Abby asked her, still curious about the coin she'd found in his cleaning bucket. She'd taken it with her, too wary about the thief running loose on the island to risk leaving it unprotected in the lab.

Wilma shook her head. "Both he and Hugo seem to be playing hooky this afternoon. I haven't seen either one of them."

Abby had stopped by Hugo's office right after lunch, but, once again, he hadn't been there. Then she'd gotten too caught up in working on the display to notice his absence.

"I've kept Wallace hopping lately getting ready for the opening," Wilma said, "so he probably deserves some time off.

But Hugo usually tells me when he's going out, so it seems strange for him just to disappear like that."

There were a lot of strange things happening on Sparrow Island that Abby couldn't seem to explain. Still, it made her wonder about Hugo's continual absences from the conservatory. Perhaps he was simply attempting to clear up these suspicions himself since Abby wasn't having much success.

"Do you suppose he'll bring her to the exhibit opening?"

Abby blinked, realizing she'd been too caught up in her own thoughts to listen to what Wilma had been saying. "Bring who?"

"The Downey woman," Wilma replied. "She hasn't called all day, which is unusual, so I just assumed that's where he went."

That possibility caused an ache deep inside of her. It was a logical assumption. Hugo was a handsome, eligible bachelor. Any woman would be thrilled to be his date.

Abby pushed aside the sadness that threatened to envelop her and focused on reason instead. The rumors that Hugo might be a con man would grow to astronomical proportions if he brought a very wealthy woman to the opening on Friday night.

Hugo would know it too. He was not only handsome, but intelligent. She doubted he'd show up with Regina Downey on his arm. As the Curator, he was more aware of the importance of his good reputation with the conservatory than anyone else on the island.

It was a reputation that would be in tatters if Abby didn't get to the bottom of this mystery.

CHAPTER ✿ ELEVEN

ON THURSDAY MORNING, Mary entered Little Flock and headed for the office. Inside she found Janet at the computer working on the Sunday church bulletin.

"Do you have time for an old friend?" Mary asked her from the doorway.

Janet turned around with a wide smile on her face. "I always have time for you! Come on in."

Mary rolled her wheelchair inside the office. The door to Rev. Hale's inner sanctum was open, but the room was dark. "Are you all alone here?"

"Rev. Hale is out visiting some homebound members," Janet explained. "So this is a perfect time for me to take a break."

Mary didn't waste any time getting to the point of her visit. The rift between two of her best friends had hit her hard. "I'm here about this problem between you and Margaret."

Janet's smile faded. "I really don't feel like talking about it."

Mary rolled her wheelchair closer to the desk. "We have to talk about it. We've all been friends for so many years. How can you let a disagreement tear you two apart? You even quit the book club!"

Tears gleamed in Janet's eyes. "It's so hard for me to explain."

"You know you can tell me anything," Mary said softly.

One tear spilled over Janet's cheek, followed by another. "She mocked me, Mary. I wanted to sing a song for my mother, and Margaret made it a joke."

That wasn't how Abby had described the tiff between them. Perhaps Janet's bruised emotions had made her twist the events of that lunch in her mind. Mary knew all too well how that could happen. After her car accident, her own feelings of fear, apprehension and despair had made her overly sensitive to the most innocent of remarks.

"It's not like you to hold a grudge for so long," Mary said gently. "You know Margaret loves you."

Janet wiped away a tear with the back of her hand. "I know she hasn't apologized for what she said to me. Not *truly* apologized, anyway."

Mary knew that sometimes an objective opinion could be very useful. She wondered if Janet had confided in Rev. Hale about her bitterness toward Margaret.

"I know you don't understand how much she hurt me," Janet said with a sniff. "You have a beautiful singing voice."

"I do understand," Mary replied, compassion for her friend almost overwhelming her. "I'm sorry that you're hurt, Janet, truly I am. I just worry that holding onto this anger against Margaret will hurt you even more."

"I'll be all right," Janet assured her with a bleak smile. "I still have you for a friend, right?"

"Always," Mary promised, reaching across the desk to squeeze her hand.

When she left the office, Mary found her way to the sanctuary of the church. She needed time alone with God to sort out her feelings and ask for His guidance. For the first time it occurred to her that Janet and Margaret might never be friends again.

As she bowed her head to pray, Mary reminded herself that it was all in His hands. Her prayers were fervent and deep. When she opened her eyes she saw a rainbow of colors reflected on the chrome trim of her wheelchair. She looked up to see the light coming from the beautiful stained glass window beside her.

A welcome serenity overcame her as she gave the burdens in her heart to the Lord. Mary knew at that moment that everything was going to be all right. He would show her the way.

BY THURSDAY AFTERNOON, Abby was ready for a break from the conservatory. She'd been working nonstop on the exhibit and noticing Hugo's absences more and more. He'd been in the office yesterday, yet offered no explanation for his mysterious disappearance on Tuesday. Feeling it wasn't her place to question him, Abby's imagination had worked overtime coming up with excuses for him—excuses that were starting to wear a little thin.

Now she stood at the front entrance of the Riley home, not far from the conservatory grounds. She was determined to put Hugo and the mystery of Howard Barnaby out of her mind for a few hours. She was awed by the size of the white colonial house. Four huge pillars bracketed the double doors. She raised the brass knocker, tapping it twice.

A moment later, the door opened and an older man wearing a tailored black suit and tie stood on the other side. His black shoes were polished to a high sheen.

Despite the comment on the invitation that formal dress wasn't necessary, Abby suddenly felt very underdressed in her yellow silk blouse and black slacks.

"Mr. Riley?" she asked as the man continued to stare at her. "I'm Abby Stanton."

"No, madam," the man replied in a deep, solemn voice. "I am Graves, the Rileys' butler. Mr. and Mrs. Riley will be having their tea in the solarium today. Please follow me."

Abby walked over the threshold and onto the gleaming white marble floor of the expansive foyer. Sunlight streamed through the windows in the vaulted ceiling, giving a burnished glow to the antique gold urns lining the wide hallway.

As she followed Graves, Abby wondered if the Rileys had experienced any thefts. They had so many valuable items displayed, both inside and outside their home, that it seemed like they would be a prime target for Sparrow Island's local thief.

Graves opened another set of doors, then stood aside so Abby could pass by him and enter the large solarium. One wall of the solarium was completely made of glass and the room itself was filled to the brim with all kinds of exotic plants and flowers. She instantly thought of her sister and hoped she'd be able to describe them accurately when she returned home.

"Mr. and Mrs. Riley will be with you shortly, madam" Graves intoned, then he disappeared from the open doorway, the echo of his shoes on the marble floor slowly fading away.

Abby moved toward the wall of glass, which looked out

over the Sound. A loon perched on a large rock near the shore, cleaning its feathers. The warmth of the sun shining through the thick pane of glass made her feel relaxed and a little sleepy.

She'd risen early this morning to catch Wallace Sibley before he started mowing the lawn in front of The Nature Museum. Her mind wandered back to their conversation and his surprise at the coin she'd found in his cleaning bucket.

Wallace had claimed he'd never seen it before and insisted that Abby keep it for herself. When she'd pondered how the coin could have ended up in his bucket, he hadn't had a clue.

Then Wallace told her that he'd been so busy getting the conservatory in shape for the Rites of Spring opening that he'd been having trouble keeping track of his equipment. He hadn't even realized he'd left the cleaning bucket outside the tool room of the laboratory.

Now Abby found herself more frustrated than ever. She still couldn't explain the sudden appearance of the two rare coins or whether they were connected to Howard Barnaby.

Or why they'd turned up in her laboratory. Had someone planted them there?

A movement outside the window caught her attention and she was surprised to see a wallaby among the lush plants in the enclosed garden. It looked just like a tiny kangaroo.

"Dr. Stanton?"

Abby turned around to see a couple standing in the doorway. They wore matching blue kaftans and the woman had a tiny capuchin monkey perched on her shoulder.

"Hello," Abby said, collecting herself. "You must be Mr. and Mrs. Riley."

The man, who was a few inches shorter than his wife,

greeted her with a wide smile. "Please call me Paul." He hurried over to shake her hand. "This is such a pleasure for both of us."

"And please call me Anne," Mrs. Riley said, moving beside her husband. "We don't stand on formality here. Well, except for Marion . . ."

". . . but he's kind enough to put up with all of our shenanigans," Paul said.

Abby found herself instantly warming to the Rileys. They might be a bit eccentric, but they were both so open and welcoming that she felt at ease in their presence.

"Marion is Anne's brother," Paul explained, "although . . ."

". . . he probably just introduced himself to you as Graves," Anne said.

Abby tried not to look surprised. "Your brother is the butler?"

Anne gave her a whimsical smile. "Graves is a very proud man. When we asked him to move in with us, he insisted that we employ him as our butler so he could earn his own way. He's been in service . . ."

". . . for a number years and is actually quite good at it." Paul chuckled. "Frankly, I think he just wanted an excuse . . ."

". . . to run our household," Anne finished for her husband. "My brother has always been extremely self-disciplined and organized, even when we were children. I'm afraid I'm the scatterbrain in the family."

"But such a beautiful scatterbrain," Paul said, "that I couldn't resist falling in love with her when she accidentally took my golf cart and . . ."

". . . ran it right into a creek," Anne said. "I was mortified, of course. Those silly golf carts all look the same."

Then she turned to her husband. "My brother also has much better manners than the two of us. Here we are talking Dr. Stanton's leg off and we haven't even asked her to sit down."

"Please call me Abby," she insisted, beginning to understand why Graves wanted to maintain some semblance of order in this house. The Rileys were so used to finishing each other's sentences that she had a little trouble keeping up with their conversation.

"Please do have a seat, Abby," Anne Riley said, motioning her to a wing chair upholstered in a striped green damask.

When the Rileys sat down on the floral loveseat opposite her, the capuchin monkey climbed off of Anne's shoulder and made its way down to the floor.

"His name is Rufus," Anne said, following Abby's gaze. "And I'm afraid he's a bit of a scatterbrain too. We were his foster parents for . . ."

". . . a fine organization in Massachusetts called the Sidekick Foundation," Paul continued. "It trains capuchins to assist quadriplegics or people with severe spinal cord injuries with everyday activities. It really is quite amazing . . ."

". . . what they can train the monkeys to do," Anne said, "but poor Rufus didn't make the cut, so . . ."

". . . we kept him." Paul smiled at his wife. "And we haven't ever regretted it. Capuchins are fascinating creatures. They're tree dwellers in the wild and can travel long distances very quickly through the trees. We . . ."

". . . absolutely love animals," Anne said with a happy sigh. "That's why we were so anxious . . ."

". . . to meet you." Paul leaned back against the sofa and crossed his legs. "Your work at the conservatory must be fascinating."

"It is," Abby agreed. "I love animals too. In fact, I noticed a wallaby in your garden."

Anne laughed. "Ah, yes. We're gathering quite a menagerie. The wallaby's name is Delilah and she's a rescue . . ."

". . . from an illegal zoo in New Jersey." Paul took his wife's hand. "We hope to place her in a sanctuary, but we haven't found the right one yet. Or maybe it's that we're . . ."

". . . just too attached to Delilah to let her go so soon." Anne turned toward the door. "Ah, it looks as if our tea has arrived."

Abby watched Graves walk into the room holding a silver tea tray, his expression dour. Though she enjoyed the Rileys, she had to admit she was ready for a break from their ping-pong style of conversation.

Rufus climbed up on Abby's chair, then sat on the arm and stared at her, his small head tilted to one side. She smiled at the adorable monkey as Anne handed her a cup of tea.

Rufus climbed higher up on her chair, then pursed his lips and blew on her tea.

"I'm so sorry," Anne said, pouring another cup of tea for her. "That was one of the skills he learned at school." Then she turned to her brother. "Marion—I mean, Graves—could you please take Rufus out with you? I think it's almost time for his nap."

"Of course," her brother intoned, gathering up the monkey. "Come along, Rufus."

"He's really all right in here," Abby told them.

Paul smiled. "You might change your mind about that when he starts dabbing your mouth with a napkin. It's another one of the skills he learned at the foundation and . . ."

". . . once he learns how to do something, he just doesn't stop."

"Will there be anything else?" Graves asked.

"No, thank you," Anne told her brother. "I think we have everything we need for now."

Graves walked out of the solarium with Rufus in his arms. After they were gone, Anne poured a cup of tea for her husband and herself.

"I'm afraid my brother gets annoyed with me when I call him by his first name. He's very strict . . ."

". . . about using the proper protocol." Paul took a sip of his tea. "Especially around guests."

Anne held out a tray of cucumber and watercress sandwiches. Abby took one, enjoying the light, delicate crunch when she took her first bite. The tea was delicious as well.

"I understand you collaborate in your writing," Abby said. "That must be interesting."

Paul and Anne looked at each other. They both started to laugh. "Interesting is one way to put it," Anne said. "Although, we do each bring something . . ."

". . . different to the process." Paul set down his teacup. "I'm the plotter in the family, so I come up with the ideas, then Anne writes the first draft. She's very creative and has a marvelous way with words."

His wife blushed at the compliment. "We're definitely a team. Paul edits the first draft and shows me where to weave in new subplots to make the story stronger. Some people believe writing a child's book is . . ."

". . . simple," Paul continued. "But children are just as discerning readers as adults. Sometimes even more so. We receive . . ."

". . . wonderful letters"—a smile lit up Anne's face—"from young people all over the world. They send us gifts too. They all have such big hearts that it makes us even more motivated to write good stories."

Abby admired their dedication, as well as the fact that they were using their talents to bring joy into the world. That was just as important as food and clothing and shelter. Books helped to feed the mind, exposing young people to new ideas and the power of the written word.

"The best part about our job," Paul said, "is that we can go on an adventure every day without ever leaving the house."

"But enough about us." Anne cradled her teacup in her hands. "You must be wondering why we invited you here this afternoon."

Abby smiled, perfectly at ease with the gregarious couple. "I'll admit it's crossed my mind, although I have been wanting to meet you."

"We were so thrilled when Naomi told us about the book club's plan to host a fundraiser for the new library wing."

"Then we learned it was a talent show and we got so excited." Paul turned to his wife. "Do you want to ask her or shall I?"

Abby smiled, certain they'd find a way to ask the question together.

"Go ahead, dear," Anne told her husband.

He cleared his throat. "Well, we'd like to perform in the talent show, but we'll certainly understand . . ."

". . . if you don't have any room left on the roster," Anne chimed in. "We certainly don't want our library gift to . . ."

". . . make you grant us any kind of special favor," Paul said. "We want to be judged on . . ."

". . . our own merits." Anne set her teacup on the tray. "Just like everybody else. We're perfectly willing to audition . . ."

"... just name the time and place."

Abby held up one hand. "There's no audition necessary. Believe it or not, we haven't had people lining up to perform in the talent show. We'll take all the volunteers we can get."

Anne clapped her hands together. "Splendid!"

"What do you plan to perform?" Abby asked them.

Paul glanced at his wife. "An original Japanese Kabuki dance. We have the costumes ..."

"... and everything else we need." Anne grinned. "I think it will be so much fun."

Abby agreed. Something told her that just having the Rileys involved would bring an energy and joy to the talent show that was sorely needed after Janet's unexpected resignation.

"I think it sounds wonderful," Abby told them. "I'll contact you very soon with more information about the show."

"We can't wait," Anne exclaimed, then refilled Abby's teacup.

BY THE TIME she returned home that evening, Abby's head was spinning. She had spent most of the afternoon with the Rileys, hearing wild tales about their travels and trying to keep up with their tag team communication style.

"THERE YOU ARE," Mary exclaimed when Abby walked into the house. "I've been waiting for you to come home."

Abby smiled at her sister. "Well, it's certainly nice to be missed. Wait until I tell you about my visit with the Rileys."

"I want to hear all about it," Mary told her as she rolled her wheelchair to the dining room table. "But first I have a surprise for you."

Abby watched Mary reach behind her to retrieve a large shopping bag. "What is it?"

Mary grinned. "A dress for the opening, with all the accessories."

Abby blinked. "You bought a dress for me?"

"I know you don't like to shop as much as I do," Mary explained. "And if you don't like the dress I'll take it right back to the store. But when I saw it today I knew it was made for you."

Mary's excitement was contagious. Abby reached for the bag and pulled out the dress inside. It was a lovely robin blue silk dress with delicate ruffles around the neckline and three-quarter-length sleeves.

"It's so beautiful," Abby breathed. "I love that fabric."

"There are shoes to match and jewelry too," Mary told her, "but try it on first and see if it fits."

Abby intended to do just that, but first she gave her sister a warm hug. "Thank you for doing this for me. It's such a wonderful surprise."

"You're welcome." Mary patted her back. "You deserve it after working so hard on the exhibit."

Abby headed to her bedroom and tried on the dress. She was still staring at herself in the mirror when she heard Mary calling out to her.

"Abby? Are you ready yet?"

She descended the stairs into the living room, then waited for her sister's reaction.

Mary's eyes widened. "Oh, Abby. You look absolutely gorgeous."

Abby knew that was an exaggeration, but she *felt* gorgeous. The dress complimented her figure and fit like a dream.

"The hem is a little too long for the shoes I bought for you," Mary said, pursing her lips, "but that's an easy fix."

"I can't wait to wear it tomorrow night," Abby said, turning in a slow circle. "It's so comfortable and light. I almost feel like I'm floating."

Mary laughed. "Well, you'd better come back to earth and take it off so it doesn't get wrinkled. We can both get into our pajamas, make some popcorn and watch an old movie. How does that sound?"

"Perfect," Abby replied as she headed back to her bedroom to change.

She was ready to relax this evening after her busy week. Her plan was to go to bed early so she could get a good night's sleep in preparation for the big opening tomorrow evening.

After taking off the dress and pulling on her pajamas, Abby retrieved the scissors from the kitchen drawer to cut the price tags off the dress. Then she noticed some stray threads around the neckline, but couldn't see them well enough to risk clipping the delicate fabric.

Mary emerged from her bedroom dressed in her own pajamas. She moved to the cupboard and took out a bag of microwave popcorn.

"One bag or two?" Mary asked her sister.

"Two," Abby replied, grabbing her bag off the counter to get the small magnifying glass she carried with her. "I was so full from the tea this afternoon that I skipped supper, but now I'm feeling too hungry to share."

"Two bags, it is." Mary pulled out another bag of popcorn. "So tell me all about your visit with the Rileys. Did you like them?"

"Yes." Abby dug through her purse. "I liked them very much." Then she looked over at Mary. "That's funny. I can't find my magnifying glass."

"When did you use it last?"

Abby pondered the question. "It must have been sometime last week. Yes, now I remember. I was reading an abstract about the changing patterns of bird migration and the print was so tiny I needed help to read. I must have left it in my office somewhere."

"You don't need it tonight, do you?" Mary asked as the popcorn bag began to expand in the microwave.

"I guess not," Abby said with a shrug. "I just wanted to use it so I could snip these tiny threads on my new dress."

"I'll take care of it when I hem the dress," Mary promised her. "Just hang it up in my closet and I'll have it ready to go by tomorrow night."

Persuaded by both her sister and the buttery smell of popcorn, Abby decided to make one last search of her bag for her errant magnifying glass. It wasn't there, but she did come across the unusual coin she'd found in Wallace's bucket.

As Mary turned her attention to dumping the first batch of popcorn into a large bowl, Abby smoothed her thumb over the surface of the old coin, wondering if it was valuable.

Then she found herself wondering if it was possible that the coins had once belonged to Vanessa Ellsworth. She was determined to find out one way or the other.

Soon the exhibit opening would be behind her, then Abby could turn her full attention to the strange mysteries now swirling around Sparrow Island.

CHAPTER ✿ TWELVE

THE NEXT MORNING, ABBY discovered a new mystery to solve at the conservatory. The first to arrive, she unlocked the door to The Nature Museum and walked into a disaster.

The Rites of Spring exhibit that she'd worked so hard on for so many weeks was in a complete shambles. The dioramas had been torn apart and flung across the room. The suspended three-dimensional timeline now dangled by one eye screw from the ceiling.

Pieces of driftwood and branches and rocks were strewn all across the floor. The chair at the reception desk was overturned and the receiver was missing from the cordless telephone base.

She stared at the damage, too shocked to move or think. Then Abby heard the door open behind her and turned to see Hugo walk inside. He looked past her, his blue eyes going wide with shock.

"What happened in here?"

"I have no idea," she breathed, her voice tight. So many hours of work ruined in one fell swoop. "I just arrived here and found all of this."

Hugo walked closer to the display, reaching down to pick up a small platform that had been turned upside down. "Who would do something like this?"

Abby didn't have an answer. The destruction seemed so random and senseless. There was no reason to destroy the exhibit. There were no valuable items to recover from beneath all the plywood and cardboard and greenery. No controversial subjects broached by the study of spring.

It simply made no sense.

Hugo looked slowly around him. "Was the door open when you arrived?"

She shook her head "No, it was locked. I used my key to get in."

He walked over to the door, opening it to examine the lock. "It doesn't look tampered with. I don't think the vandal forced his way in—at least not through this way."

"Maybe he got in through the workroom door," Abby ventured, wondering how long it would have taken to inflict all this damage.

Hugo moved closer to her. "We need to stay together, Abby. It's possible the intruder is still in here somewhere."

His words sent a spasm of fear through her. "Maybe we should call the police."

"That's an excellent idea." Hugo looked over at the reception desk. "But first we need to find the phone."

As they searched the room Abby came across the cordless telephone receiver sticking out of a box of tissues on the floor.

"Here it is," she told Hugo, pointing it out to him. "But let's use my cell phone instead. We don't want to smudge any possible fingerprints."

Abby retrieved her cell phone from her bag and handed it to Hugo. He dialed the number for the sheriff's substation.

"Hello?" Hugo said, his voice low. "This is Hugo Baron. Abby and I are over at the conservatory and it looks like there's been a break-in."

Abby leaned against the desk, her knees feeling a little shaky from the aftershock.

"Yes," Hugo said into the phone. "Okay. Thanks, we will."

He handed the cell phone back to Abby. "We're supposed to wait right here. Henry's in the neighborhood so he'll only be a few minutes."

Abby found comfort in Hugo's presence. He was so calm in the face of danger. She didn't want to imagine what might have happened if she'd caught the intruder in the act this morning. Or worse, if she had decided to retrieve her magnifying glass last night and stumbled upon him in the dark.

A shudder passed through her and Hugo laid a comforting hand on her shoulder. "Are you sure you're all right, Abby?"

"Yes," she assured him, determined not to let her imagination run wild. "I'm fine."

"I just don't understand this," Hugo said, his gaze moving over the ruined display. "Our opening is scheduled for tonight. We have hundreds of guests invited to see our newest exhibit."

"We'll have to contact them right away," Abby said. "But let's resolve right now that we're simply postponing the opening and not canceling it. We can't let some vandal scare us away from our work."

Hugo smiled down at her. "That's what I like about you, Abby. You've got gumption."

Abby smiled back at him, wishing she felt as brave as she sounded.

"I think Henry's here," Hugo said, peering out the door.

She breathed a sigh of relief when Sgt. Henry Cobb walked inside The Nature Museum.

Henry's gaze went immediately to Abby. "Are you all right?"

"Yes, I'm fine," she told him. "But as you can see, our Rites of Spring exhibit isn't doing so well."

Henry assessed the damage, then shook his head. "It looks like somebody threw a temper tantrum in here."

Abby followed his gaze, realizing that was *exactly* what it looked like. Nothing in the display was actually destroyed beyond repair, just flung about the room in a haphazard manner.

The realization that she wouldn't have to start from scratch again cheered her considerably.

Henry ordered the police officers he'd brought with him to search the rest of the museum and the outbuildings of the conservatory for any signs of the intruder.

Then he pulled out his notepad and began to question his witnesses. "Tell me exactly what you saw when you arrived here, Abby."

She took a deep breath, wanting to be as accurate as possible. "I didn't notice anything unusual until I opened the door. Then I saw the display all torn apart and I just felt sick."

"Did you hear or see anything unusual when you walked through the door? Any odd sounds?"

She shook her head. "No. I didn't even think the vandal might still be in the building until Hugo mentioned the possibility and said we had to stick together until you got here."

Henry gave her boss a nod of approval. "Good thinking, Hugo."

"I'll admit I was acting purely on instinct," Hugo said. "I

wasn't thinking too clearly when I first walked in and saw what had happened."

Henry jotted down a few notes, then asked Abby another question. "Do you have any idea who might have done this?"

"No," she exclaimed, "none at all."

"Give yourself a little time to think about it," he cautioned her. "Think back a few days or even a few weeks. Can you think of any threats made against you or the conservatory?"

She shook her head. "No, Henry, really. I would tell you if I knew of anything like that."

He glanced at her boss. "How about you, Hugo? I know you've been having some trouble with this private investigator who's been sniffing around."

"He's too busy trying to damage my reputation and career to dirty himself with this kind of work. Besides, what would he have to gain by it?"

Abby agreed with his assessment. Gary Diggs had a problem with Hugo, not her or the conservatory. Besides, this didn't seem personal. There was no hateful graffiti or violent destruction. It looked exactly like Henry had said, like somebody throwing a tantrum.

Now she just had to figure out who.

"I simply can't think of anyone who'd do something like this," she replied. "Or why. It just makes no sense."

Even more puzzling was how the intruder had entered without any sign of a break-in.

"Will you be dusting for fingerprints?" Hugo asked him.

Henry nodded. "Yes, although with the number of people coming in and out of The Nature Museum all day, we'll probably find thousands of prints. I doubt they'll be much use."

"You don't sound very optimistic about solving the case," Abby said.

Henry sighed. "I'm afraid this is going to be a tough one with so little evidence. That's why I'd like to figure out a motive that will at least lead me in the right direction."

The officers returned and notified Henry that the buildings were all clear. Abby didn't know whether to be relieved by this news or not. The way Henry talked, it would be almost impossible to apprehend the intruder unless they caught him red-handed.

After the officers left to walk the grounds, Henry turned to Hugo. "Has anything like this ever happened at the conservatory before?"

Hugo shook his head. "If it had, I would have called you."

Henry nodded, jotting some more notes as the door opened and Wilma Washburn walked inside.

Her mouth dropped open when she saw the mess in front of her. "Oh my. What happened here?"

"We're not sure," Hugo told her. "But our display is temporarily closed."

"But the opening is tonight," Wilma cried. "What are we going to do?"

"We're going to have to postpone it," Abby said. "We'll need to make a sign for the front entrance. We also might want to call the cable company and ask them to put an announcement on the local access channel. Then we'll start making phone calls to invited guests."

"All excellent ideas," Hugo replied. "Wilma, can you get that started for us?"

"Of course," she said, gathering herself once more. "I'll get right on it."

Hugo turned to Henry. "Now what can we do to help you with the investigation?"

Henry didn't hesitate. "I'll need both of you to go through

every room in this building and make a list of any items that are missing."

"So you think this might be a burglary and not just vandalism?" Abby asked him.

"I don't know what to think yet," Henry replied. "All I know is that reports about stolen items have been increasing every day."

Hugo frowned at this news. "Are you any closer to catching the thief?"

"I'm afraid not," Henry said with a sigh. "I'll admit that the case has me baffled. And I don't know if what happened here has any connection to it or not."

Abby understood his frustration. She'd been just as stymied in her own investigation into Howard Barnaby. After clearing a few possible suspects, she'd hit a dead end. Now it seemed as if her search would be even further delayed while she put the Rites of Spring exhibit back together.

Maybe that was the point.

It was a shaky motive, but the only one she had so far. Abby headed for her office, relieved to find on entering that nothing seemed to be disturbed.

She conducted a thorough inventory, including all her desk drawers and file cabinets. Everything was in order, which only made the chaos in the main hall all the more confusing.

Was it possible that she'd made enough waves to provoke Howard Barnaby into creating a diversion? That possibility seemed far-fetched, but so far she wasn't finding any other explanation.

As she emerged from her office, she found Hugo walking down the hallway.

"Anything missing?" he asked her.

"Nothing. How about you?"

Hugo shook his head. "My office looks exactly as I left it yesterday."

"So why did this happen?" Abby asked, aware that Hugo didn't have any more answers than she did.

"I wish I knew," he murmured as he squared his shoulders. "But one thing I do know is that it will not happen again. I've decided to hire a security guard to patrol the grounds and buildings at night. We've both put too much time and effort into this place to let someone destroy it."

Abby hated the idea, even if she understood it. She loved Sparrow Island's tranquility and tight-knit community. Hiring a security guard for the conservatory implied an expectation of trouble.

"It's not what I want, either," Hugo said, reading her expression. "But I'm not sure what else to do at this point. Perhaps if the vandal's caught, we can chalk it up as a one-time occurrence and carry on as before. Until then . . ."

"I understand."

They walked back to the main reception area, each caught up in their own thoughts. Abby needed to evaluate the display and assess the amount of damage. Hopefully, it wouldn't take more than a few days to put it all back together and make any needed repairs.

Henry looked up from his notebook as they approached. "There's something you should know."

"What is it?" Hugo asked.

Henry glanced at Wilma. "Why don't you tell them what you just told me."

Wilma took a deep breath. "Well, I don't know if it means anything, but there was a man here yesterday afternoon asking for Abby."

"Who was it?" Abby asked.

Wilma shook her head. "He looked like a tourist, but now I wonder . . ."

Hugo's brow furrowed. "Did he leave a name?"

"No," Wilma replied. "He told me he had a bird question and seemed somewhat irritated when I told him Abby had left for the day."

"Can you give me a description?" Henry asked her.

Wilma thought a moment. "Tall, about your height. Probably in his mid-fifties or early sixties. He had dark hair with gray at the temples and green eyes."

"It probably was just a tourist." Henry closed his notebook, then turned to Wilma. "But if this man shows up again, will you please call me?"

"Of course," Wilma promised.

The whole scene felt so unreal to Abby. She kept thinking she'd wake up and discover it was all some horrible nightmare. Worst of all, the news of the vandalism would eclipse the publicity she wanted to generate for the Rites of Spring exhibit.

Hugo looked at Henry. "Is there anything else we can do to help with the investigation?"

"Just keep your eyes and ears open for anything unusual. Hopefully, this is an isolated incident and won't happen again." Henry scratched his head. "I'd still like to know how the intruder got in here."

So would Abby. Only she, Hugo, Wilma and Wallace had keys to the conservatory buildings. Then another question popped into her mind.

"Henry," she began, trying to put it all together. "I'm wondering about these thefts on the island. Has there been any sign at all of the thief breaking into houses?"

"No," Henry replied, "that's why I think there could be a connection to this case. The difference is that nothing seems to be missing here, and those thefts didn't include this kind of vandalism."

Abby was right back where she started—with no clues and no idea where to look next. She sensed the threads of this tapestry were there for her to weave together, but every time she tried to grasp one, it slipped through her fingers.

"I think we need to close The Nature Museum this morning," Hugo announced, removing his jacket, "so we can clean up a bit before we allow the public in."

Wilma nodded, moving toward her desk. "I can make another sign for the door and call some of the volunteers to come in and help."

Abby knew she needed all the help she could get. But she was still determined not to delay the opening any longer than necessary.

"Hugo," Wilma called from her desk, "you have a phone call."

"Please take a message for me." Hugo said, rolling up his shirt sleeves.

"It's Mrs. Downey. She wants to see you as soon as possible."

Abby looked at Hugo and saw him tense. His reaction told her that Mrs. Downey wasn't just another donor to the conservatory.

"I'll be back soon," Hugo said briskly after he hung up the phone. Then he headed out the door without another word.

Wilma looked over at Abby and raised her eyebrows.

"What was that all about?" Henry asked, obviously as disconcerted by Hugo's sudden departure as the rest of them.

Everyone on Sparrow Island knew about Hugo's dedication

to the conservatory. This made it even more unusual that he'd abandon it under these circumstances.

"I don't know," Abby said truthfully.

She didn't tell Henry about the speculation that Hugo was romancing Regina Downey. Or the fact that the woman was a former movie star and now a very wealthy widow who would be the perfect target for a con man.

As if on cue, Henry changed the subject. "Any progress on your search for Howard Barnaby?"

Abby stifled a sigh. "Not much, I'm afraid. I've ruled quite a few suspects out, but there are still three or four who could be Barnaby."

"Including Hugo?"

She hesitated, hating the fact that he was a suspect at all. "Yes. I know all the circumstantial evidence seems to point to him, but I still can't believe he could be a con man."

Henry nodded, but he didn't say anything. Abby wondered if he thought she was just afraid to face the truth. Or if he trusted her instincts.

"Well, I'd better go make my report," Henry said. "Call me if you discover anything missing or come across a clue that might be important to the case."

"I will," Abby said, walking him to the door. She watched him leave in his cruiser and suddenly felt very alone. Wilma was talking on the telephone, gathering recruits to come clean up the mess that had once been the Rites of Spring exhibit.

She knew it could be recreated, but the ache inside of her just seemed to grow. The display had taken so much of her time and energy for so long that she wasn't sure she had anything left to give.

When Abby returned home that afternoon, she found her sister in the kitchen hemming her new dress.

"Don't worry," Mary said brightly, "it will be all done in time for the exhibit opening tonight."

"There's not going to be an exhibit opening—not tonight anyway."

Mary's mouth fell open. "What do you mean?"

"Someone vandalized the Rites of Spring exhibit. It's currently in pieces all over the floor of The Nature Museum."

"Oh no! Who would do such a thing?"

Abby wearily shook her head. "I don't know. Henry's investigating, but he didn't give me much hope that we'd be able to find the perpetrator."

"You worked so hard," Mary said, putting the dress aside. "I wish I could do something to make you feel better."

Her words made Abby smile. "Just the fact that I can come home and talk to you about it makes me feel better."

"I know," Mary said, snapping her fingers. "Mom's chicken soup. I think we still have a jar in the freezer."

Her mouth watered at the thought of eating her mother's delicious soup. "But I'm not sick."

"Maybe not, but you're tired and sick at heart. That's plain to see. Mom's chicken soup will make you feel better in no time."

Abby watched her sister break out the soup and begin defrosting it in the microwave. Little did Mary know that her love and support could heal her faster than anything else.

"At least now you'll have plenty of time to hem that dress," Abby said. "The exhibit opening is just on hold until we can put it back together again. I'm not sure how long that's going to take."

"You'll know when the time is right," Mary assured her. "I

was feeling impatient about putting Janet and Margaret's friendship back together until I prayed about it yesterday morning."

Abby had been so busy lately she felt like she'd been neglecting her friends. "Have you talked to either of them recently?"

Mary nodded as she carefully removed the jar of steaming soup from the microwave. "I saw Janet at Little Flock yesterday. I'm afraid nothing I said made any difference. She's still angry at Margaret and doesn't seem ready to forgive her."

"Why didn't you tell me this last night?"

Mary retrieved two bowls from the cupboard and set them on the table. "You already had so much on your mind with the exhibit opening that I didn't want to bother you with it. I also talked to Margaret."

"What did she say?" Abby grabbed two spoons from the silverware drawer.

"She's still a little miffed at Janet, but seems ready to reconcile. I suggested that she write Janet a letter of apology, but I don't know if she'll do it."

"Pride causes a lot of problems, doesn't it?" Abby mused.

Mary brought the soup to the table along with a ladle. "It sure does. I was so intent on fixing the problem between Janet and Margaret myself that I forgot to ask God for help. I always feel so much better when I remember that I don't have to face problems in life alone."

That was a reminder Abby needed too, especially today. She planned to spend some time with her Bible tonight and renew her spirit. Between that and her mother's chicken soup, she'd be ready to face anything.

CHAPTER ❦ THIRTEEN

ON SATURDAY AFTERNOON, Abby walked along the path in the woods and inhaled the fresh pine air. It had been so long since she'd gone hiking. She hadn't realized until now how very much she'd missed it.

A carpet of pine needles lay on the trail, providing a soft cushion for each step she took. The long hike was invigorating, a welcome change from the weariness that had overtaken her yesterday.

She'd spent most of this morning finishing the clean up and discovered that there was even less damage than she'd originally thought.

The opening of the Rites of Spring exhibit was now rescheduled for next Friday evening. Abby had even thought of a couple of additions to make it even better than before. She just hoped nothing else happened to interfere with their plans.

Her mind drifted to Hugo and his unexplained disappearance yesterday morning. He'd returned that afternoon, working alongside her to repair the display, but hardly said two words. That just wasn't like him.

Abby assumed that something about his visit with Mrs. Downey must have upset him. Whatever the reason, Abby hadn't asked him about it. Hugo obviously didn't want to confide in her. While that hurt a little, she respected him too much to start prying into his personal life.

When she reached the top of a hill, Abby's gaze roamed over the glorious view below her. Peace settled into her heart, giving her the comfort she sought.

She needed to make more time in her schedule for hiking. It not only renewed her, both physically and emotionally, but she'd made several interesting notes along the way to record in her birding journals.

No matter how long she lived on Sparrow Island, Abby knew she could never allow herself to take the pristine beauty of her surroundings for granted. There was nothing else like it in the world.

The sound of a twig snapping made Abby turn around just in time to see Gary Diggs walking up the path behind her.

"There you are, Abby" he said, sounding a little breathless, "I wasn't sure if I'd ever catch up with you."

"What are you doing here?"

He gave her a sheepish smile. "That's a fair question. I mean, it's not like we ran into each other accidentally. I'll admit I followed you up here. I wanted a place where we could talk privately and I figured this was as good a spot as any."

Abby disagreed. Gary's untimely arrival had spoiled her hike. Now that he was here, however, she was willing to hear him out. She knew refusing to do so would only delay the matter. His dogged stubbornness in believing that Hugo was a con man proved that he didn't give up easily.

The truth of the matter was that she was also somewhat intrigued by Gary's tireless attempts to convince her of Hugo's guilt. Why should it matter to him whether Abby was on his side or Hugo's? Unless he thought she could dig up more evidence for him. Definitive proof that he could take to the police or, more likely, a civil court to collect damages.

"It's beautiful up here," Gary said, looking around him. "I haven't really had much time to tour Sparrow Island. I've been much too busy with the case."

"Maybe you should drop the case and take a real vacation," Abby suggested. "I think it might be more productive for you in the long run."

He grinned. "Still acting as Hugo's biggest defender, I see."

"You haven't given me any reason to act otherwise. The fact that Hugo spent a month on the East Coast during the same time period that Barnaby met Vanessa Ellsworth is hardly conclusive proof of anything."

"Fair enough," Gary conceded. "Although I've come across something that's a little more persuasive. Would you like to hear it?"

She folded her arms across her chest. "I'm somewhat of a captive audience up here, Gary. So the sooner you show me what you have, the sooner I can finish my hike."

He slid his green backpack off his shoulder, then he reached inside of it and pulled out a book. The red leather spine looked vaguely familiar. He opened it to a pre-marked spot, then began to read aloud:

Everything is going well. I introduced myself to Vanessa Ellsworth today and she agreed to have dinner with me tonight. She is a lovely woman and seems eager to hear about my plan. Clarissa always said I had a way with words . . .

"What is this?" Abby breathed, uneasiness stirring inside of her.

"It's an excerpt from one of Hugo's personal journals. Would you like to hear another passage?"

Abby stared at him as Gary flipped through the pages. She couldn't believe he'd stolen Hugo's journal. Worse, he now had the audacity to read it to her.

I've stayed here long enough. Now is the perfect time to return to Sparrow Island before my absence begins to raise suspicions. I can continue my work there just as well, perhaps even more effectively. I promised Vanessa that I'd write to her often.

"That doesn't mean anything," Abby said tightly. Though she knew it wasn't true. Hugo's own words were making her begin to doubt him. He sounded so . . . calculating. So unlike the man she knew.

"Are you sure you wouldn't like to hear some of the other journal entries?" Gary asked her. "How about the one that talks about opening a post office box on the mainland? Now why do you suppose he would do that?"

"Stop," Abby demanded, then reached out her hand to take the journal away from him. "Give that to me. This is Hugo's personal property. You had no right to take it."

To her surprise, Gary handed it over without protest. "You're welcome to have it. I've already made copies of the pertinent pages anyway. The mountain of evidence that Hugo is Howard Barnaby just keeps growing. I hope you don't get hurt when it all comes tumbling down."

"I can take care of myself," she replied, her voice shaking.

But she wasn't certain if she was angry at Gary or herself. She had believed in Hugo and now . . .

"I know it's difficult," Gary said softly. "Nobody likes to be played for a fool. That's why Vanessa Ellsworth never told her family that Hugo had tricked her out of her fortune."

"Not Hugo," Abby interjected. "Howard Barnaby."

"He's one and the same."

"So now what?" Abby asked him. "Are you going to the sheriff?"

Gary hesitated. "Not quite yet."

"Then why track me down?" she challenged him. "Why make me listen to these journal excerpts? What was the point?"

Gary sighed. "I guess I'm concerned about you. Despite everything, I like you, Abby. You seem like a decent, upstanding woman."

She was surprised by the compliment, but still wary. She didn't trust Gary Diggs. The fact that he'd taken Hugo's journal had proven to her he'd do anything to make his case.

"Thank you for your concern," she said stiffly. "But it's unwarranted."

He shook his head. "You don't understand. The net is closing in on Barnaby now. He'll start getting desperate. The man you know as Hugo will panic. He'll start to act out of character."

It was already happening, but Abby wasn't going to admit that to Gary. Hugo had been so distracted lately, doing and saying things that puzzled her—like leaving the conservatory at the oddest of times. His relationship with Regina Downey also raised a red flag for her.

But none of that made him a con man, did it?

"What about the Rites of Spring exhibit?" Gary asked her.

The change of subject startled her. "What about it?"

"Don't you think the timing of the vandalism is a little strange? Some mysterious vandal breaks into the conservatory and ruins the big opening. Although, according to all of the rumors I've heard, there was no sign of a break-in. Which makes it look like it was an inside job."

All of that was true. Abby struggled within herself to stay loyal to Hugo. But Gary had a way of twisting the facts to fit his version of the truth. She couldn't listen to him anymore—not when he seemed so determined to tear down Hugo.

"I need to go," she told him, heading back down the trail.

Gary picked up his backpack, following behind her. "Just promise me you'll be careful, Abby. I don't want to be responsible if Hugo does something drastic because of my investigation."

She whirled on him. "That just proves you don't know Hugo. He is not a violent man, nor a man who acts out of desperation. I'm just sorry that you can't see that."

"Then confront him," Gary blurted.

"What?"

"Show him the passages I just read to you. Confront him with some of the incriminating statements from his own journal and see what he says. If you know him as well as you say you do, Abby, then you'll be able to see the truth in his eyes."

She stared at the man, speechless for a moment. Then she turned back around and headed down the path. Gary didn't follow her this time, much to her relief. Their conversation swirled in her head all the way back to the conservatory.

Abby knew she needed to wade through all the assumptions and innuendos to find the facts. The truth was hidden somewhere deep within the murky sea of speculation. Only Abby felt like she was treading water, too fearful of what she might find while searching for it.

Gary wanted her to confront Hugo, certain her boss would

crumble beneath her accusations. Abby was just as certain that Hugo would have a reasonable explanation for all of these incriminating circumstances that kept cropping up around him.

For instance, his trip to the East Coast during the same month Howard Barnaby met Vanessa Ellsworth; his relationship with the mysterious Regina Downey; those journal passages that Gary had read to her, which had sounded like a con man setting up his target to be fleeced.

When she reached The Nature Museum, Abby headed for her office. Wallace Sibley was inside, sweeping the floor.

"Hello, Wallace," Abby said, walking to her desk. She just wanted to gather her things and go home, too upset to work on the display this afternoon.

He looked up, surprised to see her. "I'll get out of your way, Dr. Stanton. I didn't think you'd be in on Saturday."

"Just pretend I'm not here," she advised him. "I just need to pick up a few things, then I'm headed home."

"I'm almost through here anyway," Wallace said, moving his broom more swiftly across the floor. He corralled the debris into the standing dustpan, then carried both it and the broom out of her office.

Abby watched him go, wondering if her presence made him uncomfortable. Wallace was usually more talkative. His footsteps echoed down the hallway as Abby turned her attention back to her desk.

She was almost caught up on her paperwork, but wanted to take some of it home with her so she could finish it this weekend. Sifting through the messages on her desk, she sorted them in order of priority, then gathered the notes for the article she was writing.

As she placed all the materials in her bag, she noticed Hugo's journal. Had Gary actually broken into Hugo's home to get it? She wished now that she'd asked him. He'd caught her so off guard out on the trail, that she hadn't been thinking clearly.

Fatigued from her hike and her encounter with Gary, Abby hitched her bag over her shoulder, then headed out of her office. Walking down the hallway, she was surprised to see Hugo's office door open and the man himself seated at his desk.

He looked up when she paused at the doorway. "Abby, come in. I didn't realize you were here."

"I just got back from a hike," she explained, walking inside his office. "I wanted to check on Quackers and try to make a dent in the pile on my desk."

He gave her a wry smile. "That's the same reason I'm here today. Although, a hike sounds much more tempting."

Abby knew he might change his mind about that if he ran into Gary Diggs on the trail. "I have something for you."

She reached into her bag and pulled out his missing journal.

Hugo's eyes widened as she set it on his desk. "My journal! Where did you find it?"

"Gary Diggs gave it to me. I just met him on the trail."

Hugo's gaze met hers and she saw the bewilderment there. "Why did Gary have it?"

"I'm assuming he took it," Abby said. "I'm afraid I never got around to asking him that specific question. If I were you, I'd call Henry and ask him to investigate. If Gary Diggs broke into your house and took your journal, that's a crime."

Hugo didn't say anything. He picked up the journal, running his thumb over the leather spine. "Why did he take this particular journal?"

Before Abby could reply, Hugo said, "No, don't tell me. It's the one where I talk about meeting Vanessa Ellsworth, isn't it?"

She nodded. "Gary read me a couple of passages from it. I'm sure he took them out of context."

"Are you?"

His tone was brusque and Abby felt her cheeks burn. "Of course. I know you're not Howard Barnaby."

Hugo got up and began to pace behind his desk. "You say that, Abby, but I see you looking at me differently. People are whispering behind my back. Rumors are flying about me."

"Hugo, I..."

He shook his head. "Please don't deny it. I've seen you solve mysteries before. You always face them head on, never afraid to go after the truth. But this time it's different."

He stopped pacing and looked at her. "Why?"

The question hung in the air, creating a wall between them that Abby couldn't breach. The pain she saw in his blue eyes reverberated through her.

Abby didn't know what to say. Her friendship with Hugo was on the line, but she couldn't lie to him. Those seeds of doubt kept growing in her mind. And so far, nothing he'd said had changed that.

He didn't try to defend or justify those incriminating journal passages. Neither did he explain his odd behavior these past couple of weeks. Abby wanted to believe in him, but he wasn't making it easy for her.

The silence stretched out between them, awkward and tense.

"Never mind," Hugo said at last. "You don't have to tell me."

Abby's heart ached when she saw the disappointment wash over his face. She'd let him down. Yet, he must see her dilemma. Hugo was right—she did face other investigations head on. Only this investigation pointed right at her boss. Her friend. And she couldn't face the fact that he might really be Howard Barnaby.

Hugo's gaze dropped to his desk. He began shuffling papers, leaving his journal untouched.

Abby stood there for a moment, wanting to say something —anything—to alleviate this awful tension between them. Instead, she turned around and walked out of his office, afraid any further discussion would just make things worse.

She rushed down the hallway, her eyes blurry with unshed tears. As she rounded the corner, she almost bumped into Wallace.

"Whoa," he said, catching her by the shoulders. "Are you all right, Dr. Stanton?"

She blinked back the moisture in her eyes, then gave him a nod. "Yes. I'm fine."

His face registered concern. "Are you sure? You don't look fine."

She sucked in a deep breath, trying to gather herself. "Yes, thank you."

Wallace released his grasp. "All right, then. Have a good day."

It was much too late for that. She'd let down a friend and in the process, let down herself. Like the doubting Thomas in the Bible, she wanted to see the evidence to believe it. Evidence that would exonerate Hugo once and for all.

Now their friendship might never be the same. She might even have to leave her job at the conservatory if the tension between them became too untenable.

That meant possibly leaving her sister and her parents too. Perhaps even returning to Cornell and leaving Sparrow Island behind her once more.

Abby shook that thought from her head. She couldn't even contemplate such a move at the moment. Nor did she intend to give up on Hugo so easily.

CHAPTER 🌹 FOURTEEN

THE HURT EXPRESSION ON Hugo's face kept flashing through Abby's mind as she drove to the Stanton Farm. A lump formed in her throat that she couldn't dislodge. She needed time to sort out her thoughts and yearned for the comfort and advice that only her parents could provide.

As soon as she turned into the driveway, Abby began to feel a little better. George and Ellen had raised their family on this twenty-five acres of land, giving Abby and Mary the perfect place to grow up. Although she hadn't lived on this farm for over thirty years, she still thought of it as home.

As she walked up to the back porch of the house, Abby could see Sam Arbogast, the hired farm-hand, working on the clapboard barn with several of the free-range chickens pecking the ground around him.

The screen door on the back porch opened with its familiar creak and Abby saw her mother standing on the threshold wearing a blue gingham apron and a wide smile on her face.

"Well, this is a nice surprise," Ellen said, opening the door wider to let her daughter inside.

Abby gave her mother a hug, then walked into the kitchen. George sat at the round oak table, drinking a cup of coffee. He looked just as happy to see Abby as her mother had.

"You're just in time," George announced. "Your mother has spice cookies in the oven."

Abby smiled. The scent of cookies baking took her back through the years. She and Mary had frequently come home from school to find fresh-baked cookies and a glass of cold milk waiting for them. They'd sit at the kitchen table and tell Ellen all about their day.

Her mother had perfect timing. Abby needed a cookie right now. She also needed some advice.

"Can we talk?" Abby said, taking a seat at the kitchen table.

Her mother and father exchanged glances.

"Of course," George said. "Is something wrong?"

She hesitated, not certain how to begin. Ellen sat down at the table next to Abby, placing a gentle hand on her forearm.

"Is this about Hugo?" Ellen asked her.

Abby glanced up at her. "How did you know?"

"We've heard the rumors," George explained. "I even met that private detective once on Shoreline Drive. He asked me for any information I might have about Hugo. I told Mr. Diggs that the only thing he needed to know was that he was on a wild goose chase."

Abby sighed. "At least you stuck up for Hugo. I let him down."

"Abby," Ellen admonished, "I'm sure that can't be true."

"It is," Abby countered, her throat tight.

The oven timer dinged. Ellen gave her arm a warm squeeze before she got up to take the cookies out of the oven. When she returned to the table, she brought a glass of milk for Abby and a plate of cookies.

"Here," George said, handing her a cookie, "this will make you feel better."

Abby laughed in spite of herself. In her father's mind, Ellen's cookies could solve most of life's problems. As she took a bite of the warm, chewy cookie, Abby wondered if there might be some truth to it.

"Now," Ellen said, cradling her coffee cup in her hands, "why don't you tell us all about it?"

Secure in the comfort of her family home and the love of her parents, Abby started to tell them the story from her first meeting with Gary Diggs. They nodded as she spoke, but let her talk without interruption.

"When I heard the passages from his journal about Vanessa Ellsworth, I didn't know what to think," Abby told them. "If the journal had belonged to anyone but Hugo, those passages would have made the writer my prime suspect."

"But you know Hugo isn't capable of that kind of deception," George said.

Abby met his kind gaze. "I thought I knew it, but now . . ."

"What, dear?" Ellen prodded.

"I ran into Hugo at The Nature Museum this afternoon and now he knows that I have doubts about him. If you had seen the look on his face . . ."

George handed her another cookie. "Do you believe he's a con man?"

"Of course not," Abby said vehemently. "I believe in my

heart that he's innocent, but my head keeps trying to make sense of everything and it's not working. There are so many unanswered questions."

Ellen leaned back in her chair. "Have you asked Hugo these questions?"

Abby shook her head. "No, I can't ask him. That would be giving credence to the suspicions that he's Howard Barnaby."

For a long moment, the only sound was the loud report of a hammer against wood through the open window as Sam repaired the barn. Abby could feel her parents' love surrounding and supporting her. Even without words, they were making her feel stronger and helping her see the answer.

"But by not asking him," Abby said slowly, "Hugo must think I actually believe some of the accusations. We haven't talked about my investigation of Howard Barnaby for over a week now. Or rather, I've been avoiding the subject." She sighed. "And avoiding Hugo."

"It hurts when people don't believe in us," Ellen said softly. "It hurts even more when those people are our friends."

Her words reminded Abby of the rift between Janet and Margaret. It had all started when Margaret suggested Janet might embarrass herself by singing in public. Margaret hadn't believed in her talent, so Janet had struck back with an insult about Margaret's baking and it had all escalated from there.

Their dispute wasn't about singing or baking. It was about trust and loyalty. About believing in your friends, even when doubts surfaced.

Abby owed Hugo that same trust and loyalty. He'd always stood by her. Now she needed to do the same. Instead of excluding him from her investigation of Howard Barnaby, she was going to lay all the facts out on the table and let him explain his relationship with Vanessa Ellsworth. She was going to ask him about Regina Downey too. No more secrets between them.

Their friendship was too important to let fear and doubt erode it.

"Thank you," Abby told her parents. "I feel so much better."

George chuckled. "I'm not sure we were much help to you."

"You were," she assured him. "More than you'll ever know."

"God can always help too," Ellen reminded her. "Shall we pray together?"

They joined hands and bowed their heads.

"Heavenly Father," George prayed, "please guide Abby as she searches for the truth. Let her faith carry her through and give her the strength of heart to find the answers she seeks. Be with her, Lord, and protect her. Amen."

"Amen," Abby and Ellen chorused together.

Abby squeezed both of their hands before she let them go. Coming to the farm today had been one of the best decisions she'd made lately. From now on, she wasn't going to let fear keep her from seeking answers.

"How about another cookie?" Ellen offered.

Abby laughed. "I've had two already, but I'll take some home for Mary."

"I'll wrap some up," Ellen said.

George smiled at his daughter. "I bought tickets for the talent show today. Sounds like it's going to be a packed house."

That reminded her that she still needed to find more performers for the show, which was only a week away. At least that task now seemed like a challenge instead of a chore.

"I'd better go," she said, rising from her chair. "I still have a lot to do today."

"Here are the cookies," Ellen said, handing her the warm package. "Please let us know if you need anything else."

"I will," she promised them. But Abby already had everything she needed—her faith in God and the love of her family.

Now all she wanted was to prove to Hugo that she truly did believe in him.

ABBY STOPPED at the grocery store after her visit with her parents. It was her turn to fix dinner tonight and she needed to pick up a few items. Thanks to her mother's cookies, she didn't have to make dessert.

She walked inside The Green Grocer and grabbed a cart. In the mood for some good comfort food to go along with her mother's spice cookies, Abby had decided to make tuna noodle casserole for dinner tonight, along with Italian rolls and a salad.

As she headed down the produce aisle, Abby recognized a familiar face. "Hello, Edmonia."

Her hairdresser turned around and smiled at her. "Oh, hello, Abby."

Standing next to Edmonia was a tall gentleman with silver hair and ice blue eyes. Abby assumed it must be Edmonia's new boyfriend.

"This is Roman Dietz," Edmonia said, placing one hand on his shoulder. "Roman, this is Dr. Abby Stanton. She's one of my clients and a good friend."

Roman held out his hand. "Nice to meet you, Dr. Stanton."

"Now, now," Edmonia admonished him with a smile, "no such formalities are necessary. First names only among friends."

Abby shook his hand. "It's a pleasure to meet you, Roman."

Edmonia moved her cart closer to Abby. "Just so you know, there's a special on Kari's Creams today, four for a dollar.

They're almost gone, so I'd head straight to the bakery department if I were you."

Abby liked the flaky pastries as much as anyone, but at the moment she was much more interested in Roman—if that was his real name. "How long have you lived on Sparrow Island, Roman?"

"Just a few months," he replied. "I run a computer business out of my home, so I can live almost anywhere. After a vacation here last summer, I decided I liked it well enough to live here full time."

"He's a computer whiz," Edmonia gushed. "He updated all of the accounting programs for my business and gave me some great investment tips."

Roman laughed. "I think you're exaggerating a bit, my dear. You're the one with all the talent. I've never had a better haircut in my life."

"Is that how the two of you met?" Abby asked him, remembering that Edmonia had mentioned something about it. "You just walked into the Silver Scissors one day for a haircut?"

Roman glanced at Edmonia. "Actually, our computers brought us together. I noticed Edmonia's profile on a dating site and e-mailed her."

Edmonia blushed. "I thought we were going to keep that a secret, Roman."

Abby could see that she was embarrassed. She remembered Edmonia's odd mood at the book club meeting a couple of weeks ago. She had seemed so lonely. Maybe that loneliness had compelled her to seek love in cyberspace.

Obviously it had worked.

But what did Edmonia really know about Roman Dietz? Could he be trusted?

"We've got nothing to be ashamed of," Roman told his girl-friend. "Computer dating is just the modern version of courtship by mail. If it was good enough for the pioneers, it's good enough for us."

Edmonia laughed, then turned to Abby. "Now do you see why I like him so much? He can put a good spin on anything."

That's what worried Abby. Roman might be a perfectly nice gentleman. Or he might be a con man planning to scam Edmonia out of her money and property. As a successful busi-nesswoman, the hairdresser probably appeared like a pretty ripe plum for plucking.

Perhaps Roman had been scanning the dating site looking for wealthy women. There was no way to know for certain. That's what made Abby's search for the real Howard Barnaby so frustrating. There were too many unanswered questions.

"So are you a medical doctor?" Roman asked Abby.

"No," she replied, somewhat used to that question by now. "I'm an ornithologist."

"Abby works as the Associate Curator at the Sparrow Island Nature Conservatory," Edmonia added.

"Really?" Roman gave a slow nod. "That's a place I intend to visit soon. I've become quite interested in wildlife since moving to Sparrow Island. What fascinates me the most are the preda-tors, like hawks and eagles. Even some of the marine life stalk their prey, don't they?"

"Yes," she replied, a bit unnerved by his interest in the sub-ject. Judging by Edmonia's glowing countenance, she didn't share Abby's unease. "Orcas feed on fish, squid and other marine animals. Some of them even slide onto the shore to scare seals into the water where other orcas are waiting to feed."

"Now that's something I'd like to see," Roman exclaimed.

Edmonia wrinkled her nose. "It sounds rather gruesome to me."

He circled an arm around her shoulders. "Don't worry, my dear. I won't make you watch."

The man was a little creepy in Abby's opinion. She wondered how Edmonia didn't see it. Or maybe she was so desperate for love that she simply chose to overlook some of his flaws. Whatever the reason, Abby wanted to learn more about Roman Dietz before she crossed him off her suspect list.

"Oh, by the way," Edmonia said, looking at Abby. "I had an appointment cancel this Monday afternoon if you'd still like to come in. Now that the opening's been postponed, you'll have time to get your hair cut."

"That sounds perfect," Abby replied, making a mental note on her schedule. "I hope you're coming to the Rites of Spring opening."

Edmonia glanced up at Roman. "We wouldn't miss it, would we, honey?"

"I've already had my tuxedo pressed so it's ready to wear," he replied. "It will be my first formal occasion on Sparrow Island."

It intrigued her that a man who worked from home owned a tuxedo. She wondered what kind of formal occasions he'd attended on the mainland and how many involved wealthy widows.

But Abby was getting ahead of herself. She didn't want to make the mistake of judging him after just one meeting. Something bothered her about the man, but she might be so eager to find Howard Barnaby that she wasn't giving Roman a fair chance.

"I look forward to seeing both of you there," she said sincerely. "Have a nice weekend."

"You too." Edmonia started pushing her cart down the aisle, Roman following close behind her. "See you on Monday."

Abby resumed her shopping, bypassing the bakery department, despite the temptation to sample one of Kari's Creams.

Despite some of her lingering doubts about Hugo, she'd decided to follow her heart instead of her head. Her instincts and everything she knew about the man told her that Hugo was good, decent and honorable. Those were not the traits of a con man.

Those instincts might not be good enough evidence for Gary Diggs, but they were good enough for her. She intended to let Hugo know that she believed in him the next time she saw him. She just hoped it wouldn't be too late to mend the rift in their friendship.

When Abby reached the checkout lane, she placed her items on the conveyer belt. Archie Goodfellow, the owner of The Green Grocer, was at the cash register.

"Hello, Archie," she said, reaching inside her bag for her checkbook. "Are you having a nice weekend?"

"Not much nice about it," he grumbled. "One of my checkers didn't show up for work today. Teenagers these days just don't have the same work ethic as they did when I was that age."

Abby smiled to herself, certain that exact same complaint had been echoed for generations. "Well, I hope the next few days go better for you."

"I doubt it," Archie said, used to looking on the dark side of life. "The Green Harbor town council's talking about holding a special meeting."

"Really?" Abby handed him a check for the amount on the cash register. "What about?"

"All that funny business about Hugo Baron. Some people think we should do something about it."

His words chilled her. By funny business, did he mean the rumors that Hugo was a con man?

Archie finished bagging her groceries, then handed the bag to Abby. "But you probably know about that better than anyone, since you work with the man."

"You've got it all wrong," Abby said, determined to start setting the record straight. "Hugo isn't involved in any funny business. He's responsible for creating the conservatory and bringing hundreds of tourists to Sparrow Island."

"Maybe," Archie conceded, "but that might start to change if word gets out he's some kind of scam artist. Too many businesses around here depend on those tourists to take the risk."

Frustrated by this turn of events, Abby left the store, now more determined than ever to put a stop to this nonsense once and for all.

THAT EVENING, Abby sat on the deck with a library book open on her lap. Her fruitless Internet research of Howard Barnaby had led her to an autobiography of another con man with the same modus operandi. She hoped his story might give her some clues to help her identify Barnaby.

As she read aloud, Finnegan romped in the backyard. Mary was inside the house working on one of her many craft projects.

Most of the victims of a con artist share common traits. They tend to be older women who live alone and don't have a lot of social contacts.

That made sense and fit the profile of Howard Barnaby's victims.

While many con men use an alias, you can usually find some clue to their identity in their phony name. It may be connected to the street they grew up on, the name of their elementary school, or even a town or place that is important to them.

The fact that his name probably had significance for him did offer her a lead she hadn't considered before. She'd assumed Barnaby had just plucked his pseudonym from thin air. It was a weak clue, but a clue nonetheless.

If she gathered background information of all the men she suspected, it might point her in the right direction.

Abby turned back to the book, fascinated by the author's cool recollections of his life of crime.

If you lined up a group of people in a room, even the most skilled detective wouldn't be able to pick out the con artist right away. He's too good at fooling people and playing innocent. If a con man thinks the heat is on, he'll go underground until the coast is clear.

Abby sighed. If the real Howard Barnaby knew about Gary Diggs's investigation, she might never find him. He might stay in hiding until someone else took the fall for his crimes.

Finnegan ran up to her and dropped his favorite tennis ball at her feet.

"Oh, Finnegan," she said with a sigh. "I wish I knew all the answers."

He cocked his head to one side as if waiting for her to tell him her problems.

Smiling, Abby picked up his tennis ball and tossed it into the yard. The dog bounded after it, his tail wagging.

She turned to the last page of the chapter, hoping to find more glimmers of information that would help her search.

If you suspect you're being conned by a pro, look at the people closest to you. Chances are it's someone who's earned your trust and is now abusing it. The one piece of advice I have for people out there is: Trust no one.

Abby closed the book, saddened that anyone could have that kind of outlook on life. Yet, she knew that's how she needed to conduct this investigation. From now on she intended to follow the facts instead of her feelings. Hugo had told her as much when he'd accused her of holding back her investigation because of their friendship.

It was a friendship she hoped wasn't over.

CHAPTER ❧ FIFTEEN

On MONDAY MORNING, Abby stopped by Al's Garage on her way to work. He'd left a message on the answering machine that he'd received the report about her flat tire from the manufacturer and wanted her to stop by.

Abby thought it a little strange that he wanted to see her in person instead of just telling her about it over the phone, but she liked Al and trusted him as a mechanic. If he wanted to see her in person, it must be about something important.

She parked her car in the lot, then walked into the office where the heavy scent of pine deodorizer masked the pungent oil fumes. Al's wife, Laverne, sat behind the service desk.

"Hello, Abby," Laverne greeted her, setting down her pen. "Al's inside the service area. You can just go on in."

Abby walked through the steel door that separated the office and the service area. She saw Al hunched over the open hood of a vintage Mustang and waited until he finished checking the oil before approaching him.

"Hi, Al."

He looked up and reached for a rag to wipe the grease off his hands. "Hey there, Abby. Thanks for coming down."

Al walked over to her, fresh grease stains marring his blue coveralls.

"I just got the report back from the tire manufacturer," Al told her, tossing the rag aside. "The bad news is that they won't cover the cost of replacing the tire."

"So it wasn't defective?"

He shook his head. "Worse, I'm afraid. According to their tests, it seems that the tire was sliced all the way through by a sharp metal object."

"What on earth could do that?"

He met her gaze. "A knife."

She stared at him. "Are you saying someone slashed my tire on purpose?"

"That was the conclusion of the report. After looking over the tire again myself, I have to agree. The slice is too clean to be caused by road debris, such as a nail or even a piece of scrap metal."

"But who would do such a thing?"

He shrugged. "I don't know, Abby, but I thought I should warn you in case it happens again. You might want to let the police know too. I'll be happy to give them a copy of the manufacturer's report."

Abby thought back to the day of her flat tire and how Gary Diggs had suddenly appeared out of nowhere to help her. At the time, she'd thought him a knight on a shiny bicycle. Now she wondered if he'd orchestrated it all from the beginning.

Had it just been a coincidence that Gary had been in the

bushes when that little boy was lost? Or had he been hiding there after he'd slashed her tire and emerged when he heard them start to organize a search for the missing toddler?

The pieces fit, though she didn't understand the motivation behind his actions. For some reason, it was very important to him to earn Abby's confidence.

"Abby?" Al said, giving her a quizzical look. "Are you all right?"

She blinked, startled out of her reverie. "Yes, I'm fine."

The service door opened and Laverne walked into the garage. "Al, you have a phone call. It's about that part for the Corvette that you've been looking for."

His eyes lit up. "Abby, do you mind if I take this phone call?"

"Not at all," she said, knowing his love of cars. It always pleased her to see someone who took such joy in their work.

Al disappeared into the office, leaving her alone with his wife.

Laverne snatched the soiled rag off the floor and dropped it into the laundry bin. "I read about the talent show in last week's *Birdcall*. It sounds like it will be a good time."

"I hope so," Abby replied, her mind still on Gary's treachery. "Are you planning to come?"

"Absolutely." Laverne glanced at the service door, then moved a step closer to Abby. "Has Al said anything to you about volunteering?"

"No," she replied, though she wasn't surprised. The Minskys liked to contribute to the community. "I suppose we can always use some more help backstage."

Laverne hesitated. "Actually, I think he wants to volunteer to perform *onstage*."

Abby looked at her in surprise. "Al?"

Laverne laughed at her reaction. "Yes, Al. Believe it or not, my husband plays a mean violin."

Abby had to admit she did find it hard to believe. She knew Al's skilled hands allowed him to fix intricate motors and electrical systems. She just never imagined them holding a violin and delicate bow.

"Do you have room for him?" Laverne asked, hope shining in her brown eyes. "I know he's too shy to ask you himself, but he'd love to perform. He practices every day and is quite good."

"We'd love to have him," Abby said sincerely. This talent show was allowing her to look at some of the residents of Sparrow Island in a whole new light. She couldn't wait to see all of these diverse talents on display.

Laverne's face lit up. "Really? Oh, I know he'll be thrilled. Now I'm more excited about the talent show than ever!"

So was Abby. The only cloud over the event was the rift between Janet and Margaret. They still weren't speaking to each other and Janet hadn't withdrawn her resignation as president of the book club or codirector of the talent show. At this late date, it looked like she never would.

Al walked back into the garage. "Sorry I took so long, Abby."

"No problem," she replied. "It gave me a chance to chat with your wife and sign you up to perform at the talent show."

Al looked chagrined. "Laverne, you didn't."

"I did," she said proudly. "You belong on that stage, Al Minsky. Everybody on Sparrow Island should know that you can do more with your hands than rebuild a carburetor."

Abby agreed. "We look forward to having you. I'll let you know what time you need to be at the Community Center on Saturday."

She had a busy weekend ahead with the opening of the Rites of Spring exhibit scheduled for Friday, the day before the talent show.

Al grinned. "Thanks, Abby. I guess I'm looking forward to it too." Then he pulled a sheet of paper out of his pocket. "Here's a copy of the tire manufacturer's report in case you decide you want to turn it over to the police."

"I think you should," Laverne said. Al had obviously filled her in on the results before Abby's arrival. "If that tire had blown out instead of just going flat, you could have had an accident."

Abby thought of her sister, who'd lost the use of her legs in a car accident. She wasn't eager to share the report with Mary, remembering her anxiety when Abby had returned home late the other evening.

"Thank you," she told Al, taking the report from him. She wasn't certain going to the police would do any good at this point, although she might mention it to Henry the next time she saw him. She suspected Gary Diggs of deliberately slashing her tire, but she had no proof. The last thing she wanted to do was accuse him on circumstantial evidence as he was doing to Hugo.

Abby left the garage, eager to arrive at the conservatory so she could apologize to Hugo. She'd thought about their conversation all weekend and prayed about it in church yesterday. Now that she'd resolved to tell him her concerns, she didn't want to wait any longer.

To Abby's surprise, Hugo was waiting in her office when she walked through the door. "Oh, hello."

He rose out of the chair, smoothing the fabric of his tailored suit. It was the navy blue one and she wondered if he remembered that it was a favorite of hers. "Hello, Abby. I hope you don't mind me waiting in here for you."

"Not at all," she assured him, setting her bag on top of the desk.

"I wanted to catch you before we both got too busy to talk." He waited until she sat down in her chair, then resumed his seat. "I want to apologize for my behavior on Saturday, Abby. I overreacted and I'd like to ask for your forgiveness."

His words touched her, though she felt he was being much too hard on himself. "I'm the one who should be apologizing to you. In fact, I've been waiting all weekend to tell you how very sorry I am for doubting you."

He smiled. "So it seems we both regret what happened on Saturday."

"I know I do," she said earnestly. "Hugo, you must realize how much I admire you. I'll admit that Gary Diggs has managed to raise some small doubts in my mind, but I believe in you and I hope you'll give me another chance to prove I deserve your friendship."

His smile softened. "You have nothing to prove, Abby. Some people say that faith is forged by overcoming doubts, so perhaps friendship is too. At this moment, I feel that our friendship is stronger than ever."

She blushed. "So do I."

"Then I think now would be a very good time for you to ask me those questions that I know you've been wanting to ask."

Her admiration of him soared in that moment. He was truly one of the strongest men she knew. "The evidence Gary Diggs is gathering against you seems to be purely circumstantial, but I have to admit it's also fairly convincing."

"Go on."

"First, there's the fact that you visited the East Coast and met Vanessa Ellsworth during the same time period as Howard Barnaby. Vanessa mentioned a long correspondence with Howard Barnaby to her family, though they never saw any of the letters. What they did find was several canceled checks made out to the Sparrow Island Nature Conservatory."

It was more difficult to lay out the facts than Abby expected. She just hoped Hugo didn't take offense as she made the case against him.

"I can see where my conduct must look suspicious," he said at last. "All I can tell you is that I did meet Vanessa in Massachusetts five years ago, but I never passed myself off as Howard Barnaby."

"Did she ever mention him to you?"

He thought about it for a moment, then shook his head. "Not that I recall. You have to understand that Vanessa was a very gregarious woman. She had a lot of friends and corresponded with many of them."

Gary hadn't mentioned that about Mrs. Ellsworth. Abby wondered what else he'd omitted. "Do you have a post office box on the mainland?"

"No," Hugo said without hesitation.

"Have you ever had one?"

"Never. You can check with the post office if you like, although I'm not certain they can give out that information even if they have my permission."

That didn't jell with Gary's assertion about the post office box, but she'd noticed he hadn't read her that passage either. Perhaps he'd misunderstood it or had purposely tried to mislead her.

She hesitated to ask Hugo the next question, fearing it was

too personal. But his encouraging smile made her take the leap. "Gary Diggs bases his theory that you're Howard Barnaby on the fact that you seem to have a lot of disposable cash. He pointed out that you've always had enough money to travel extensively with no visible means of employment."

Hugo cocked his head. "Did he now?"

She nodded. "I know it's none of my business—"

"Yes, it is," Hugo interjected. "If you want to find Howard Barnaby, then you need to exclude all the other suspects. Like it or not, I am a suspect. Actually, the prime suspect, according to Gary Diggs."

Abby already knew about his fallout with his father. A young teenager embarking on his own in the world didn't have much chance of making a fortune. Abby didn't even know if Hugo had attended college, though he was one of the most learned men of her acquaintance.

"I received a small inheritance from my family, but most of the money belonged to my wife," Hugo said at last. "Clarissa came from a wealthy family. After she inherited, we donated most of it to charity, keeping just enough to allow us to travel around the world. We earned our keep by working at several missions along the way. It gave us an opportunity to learn about people of different cultures and their way of life, as well as a chance to share our faith with them."

His answers lifted the burdens from her heart one by one. Hugo didn't hesitate or try to justify any of his answers. Gary Diggs might suggest that a con man knew how to manipulate a conversation to make himself look good. But at this moment, Abby didn't care about Gary's opinion or his allegations. Hugo had already proved to be a true friend and that was good enough for Abby.

"You probably want to know about my journal entries," Hugo said, anticipating her next question.

"They did seem . . . odd."

He nodded. "That's because I believe Gary probably took them out of context. I want you to take my journal home and read it for yourself." Pulling open his jacket, he extracted the thin volume from his inner pocket and held it out to her.

"I don't need to read your journal to believe you," she protested.

"Then just read those specific passages. I'll feel better knowing you've read the entire entry instead of the pieces that Gary hand-picked for you."

Abby reluctantly took the journal he offered, which seemed proof enough if he was willing to let her read every entry from that year. "Thank you."

"Do you have any more questions for me?" he asked.

She saw the relief in his expression and was so glad that they'd finally gotten everything out in the open.

Well, almost everything.

"Just one more question." She took a deep breath. "What is your relationship with Regina Downey?"

Hugo's jaw sagged, the question catching him off guard. Then he cleared his throat. "I'm sorry, Abby. That's the one question that I can't answer for you."

She wanted to explain herself, just to clarify that she was asking to clear up her investigation and not for personal reasons. "I know that Regina was the movie star Regina Wilder at one time and is now a very wealthy widow. Her frequent telephone calls here and your trips to the mainland have led some people to speculate that Howard Barnaby's trying to con another woman."

To her surprise, he smiled. "Some people will believe any-thing. That's something I learned in my travels. But I can tell you honestly, Abby, that I've never conned anyone in my life and I'm not about to start now."

Abby had to be satisfied with his answer as it was obvious he wasn't going to elaborate on his connection to Regina Downey. "Thank you, Hugo. I feel so much better now."

"So do I," he replied. He stood up and rubbed his hands together. "Now on to a more cheerful subject. We have the exhibit opening in just five more days. Are we ready?'

"Very close. I need to put a few finishing touches on the display, but I believe it's even better than it was before."

"Wonderful."

Abby didn't want him to leave yet. She still had one addi-tional question to ask him. A question that had nothing to do with Howard Barnaby. "Would you consider performing in the talent show?"

His eyes widened. "Me? I don't have any talent."

She laughed. "Says the man who practically built this con-servatory and The Nature Museum with his bare hands."

"I used my head and my heart more than my hands," he admitted, "but that's not exactly the kind of talent that people pay good money to see."

"Actually, I was hoping you'd perform some of your bird-calls. You're quite proficient at them and I think it would tie in nicely with the conservatory."

He considered her idea. "I suppose I could give it a try."

"Then I'm adding your name to the list of performers," she said, before he had a chance to change his mind.

"Are you certain you want me on that stage? With all these rumors going around about me—"

Abby held up a hand to stop him. "Of course we want you. I think you'll be the hit of the show."

He sighed. "Well, either way, I'll give the crowd something to talk about."

Abby walked him to the door. Upon opening it, she saw Wallace crouched not even a foot away, turning a screw in an outlet cover near the floor.

The caretaker looked up as they emerged from Abby's office. "Seems like there's quite a few loose screws around here. I've been going around the building and tightening them all up."

Hugo nodded. "Keep up the good work, Wallace." Then he headed down the hallway to his office.

Wallace rose to his feet, groaning at the effort. "These old knees of mine aren't as flexible as they used to be. Guess that's what happens when you don't take good care of yourself. I should try to get more exercise like you do, Dr. Stanton."

She didn't reply, alarms going off in her head. Wallace had been right outside the door, no doubt able to hear every word of their conversation. She'd bumped into him at other times too. He always seemed to be just around the corner.

Perhaps it was just a coincidence, but from now on she was going to keep a closer eye on Wallace Sibley.

CHAPTER 🥀 SIXTEEN

LATER THAT AFTERNOON, Abby made time to sneak away from the conservatory for her hair appointment. The Silver Scissors was full of customers, but Edmonia had the chair ready for Abby when she walked through the door.

"How are you today?" Edmonia asked as she waited for Abby to sit down. She wrapped a blue nylon cape around her to keep hair clippings off her clothes.

"I'm just fine. It looks like things are really hopping here."

"They sure are," Edmonia spritzed her hair with water. "Roman came up with some great promotional ideas for my business. It looks like they're really paying off. If this keeps up, I may have to hire a second assistant."

Abby closed her eyes as Edmonia ran a comb through her short brown hair.

"What shall we do today?" Edmonia asked her. "Just a trim or do you want to try something really daring? Perhaps some purple and gold highlights to celebrate the big opening?"

Abby opened her eyes to see Edmonia grinning at her in the mirror. "Just a trim, please," she said with a smile. Abby couldn't even imagine what Hugo's reaction would be if she showed up to the opening with purple highlights in her hair.

Edmonia began to hum softly as she started cutting her hair, but Abby could still hear Hugo's name mentioned from the hair station next to her.

"I just don't think it's right," the customer muttered. "The town council has no authority over the conservatory, do they? So how can they tell them what to do?"

"I don't know how it all works," Glenda, Edmonia's assistant, replied. "I doubt they can force Hugo out even if they wanted to. Besides, this isn't a formal hearing. Some of the members just want to meet to discuss the issue."

"I heard they're going to try to convince him to temporarily step down as Curator for the good of Sparrow Island."

Abby couldn't believe her ears. Then she remembered Archie Goodfellow's comment about a special town council meeting to discuss the accusations against Hugo.

"Well, they are supposed to represent the voters," Glenda replied to her client. "Maybe they've been getting calls from concerned citizens."

"More like concerned busybodies if you ask me," her client replied. "It seems some people just aren't happy unless they're stirring up trouble."

"You're right," Glenda said, giving Abby hope that not everyone on the island believed the rumors. "They shouldn't even get involved. If Hugo is a con man, then he'll be arrested. If not, then why disrupt the conservatory when everything is going so well over there?"

"You're absolutely right," said her client. "We even have

tickets for the exhibit opening this Friday night. If Hugo stepped down as Curator, they might cancel the event and we'd be out ten dollars."

Abby bit her tongue, knowing it wasn't polite to join in the conversation. She wanted to defend Hugo and let them know that he wasn't a con man, but this wasn't the time or the place.

"Do you know what else I heard?" Glenda asked her client.

Edmonia turned on the blow dryer, drowning out the rest of Glenda's conversation. Abby knew it was just as well. She didn't like to eavesdrop, even knowing it was impossible to keep from hearing others converse in such close quarters.

She closed her eyes again, ruminating on the conversation she'd just heard. Surely the town council wouldn't ask Hugo to step down as Curator, even temporarily, over a bunch of baseless accusations. He wasn't even charged with a crime.

The blow dryer turned off, then Edmonia asked her, "Is this short enough, Abby?"

Abby opened her eyes and saw her reflection in the mirror. Her cheeks were flushed and her mouth drawn down into a frown. Taking a deep breath, she let the tension ease out of her. "Yes, it's just right."

"Then you're all set." Edmonia removed the cape, shaking the hair clippings to the floor. She took a small, clean paint brush and feathered it over Abby's neck to remove any stray hairs.

"Will I see you at the meeting tonight?" Abby asked her. "We've still got a lot of work to do to prepare for the talent show."

"You bet," Edmonia replied. "If I'm doing the makeup for the performers I need to make sure we have the right lighting set up."

"There are so many little details to worry about," Abby mused, thinking of both the fundraiser and the Rites of Spring exhibit.

"There sure are. Putting on this talent show is an even bigger project than I imagined. It'll be nice to get back to our book discussions."

"It will," Abby agreed. "Have you started next month's book yet?"

Edmonia grinned. "I'm almost done with it. Jane Austen's one of my favorite authors. I wouldn't miss that meeting for anything."

The book club had chosen *Persuasion*, one of Austen's lesser known works for next month's selection. Abby hadn't even opened the book yet, too caught up in the exhibit opening and her search for Howard Barnaby to do any reading.

"Guess what Roman's doing for me?" Edmonia said as Abby rose out of the chair.

"What?"

"Well, he knows how much I love Jane Austen, so he's cooking a romantic dinner for the two of us tonight. He's making all authentic Victorian period food, too, just like Jane Austen used to eat."

Abby gave Roman points for creativity. It seemed he knew the perfect recipe for how to sweep a woman off her feet. "That sounds lovely."

Edmonia walked over to the cash register to make change for Abby. "I'm sure it will be. Roman's a great cook. In fact, he's so good at everything that I sometimes wonder what he sees in me."

Though Edmonia's tone was lighthearted, Abby could hear

the insecurity underneath it. "I'm sure you have many qualities that Roman likes."

The hairdresser grinned. "He did mention that I'm a great conversationalist. Of course, working in this place all day gives me plenty of practice."

"I'm glad you found someone," Abby told her, even though she worried that Roman might not be as perfect as he seemed. "Just take it slow and enjoy yourself. After all, you've only known each other for a short while."

"It's only been about two weeks since we met in person." She wrinkled her nose. "Funny how it seems so much longer."

"That's because you've been learning so much about each other," Abby said, then laughed. "Listen to me! As if I'm an expert in love and romance."

"Well, you are," Edmonia teased, "at least regarding love and romance for the avian species."

Abby left the beauty shop feeling better about her hair and worse about Hugo's predicament. The town council had no right to ask him to resign as Curator, but even the request might be enough for Hugo to temporarily step down. The welfare of the community was important to him, even if it meant sacrificing his own career.

Of course, it was possible the town council members wouldn't agree that Hugo needed to step down. They were a diverse group, each with their own opinion. She mulled over each member, trying to guess how he or she might vote.

Frank Holloway would probably vote in Hugo's favor. Not only because they had a good relationship, but because the hardware store didn't cater to many tourists. Ana Dominquez, on the other hand, owned a craft store. However, Abby knew she was a woman of integrity and would vote with her head and not her pocketbook.

The other town council members were business owners too. Ed Willoughby owned the pharmacy, Archie owned The Green Grocer and Keith Gordon ran The Dorset. The tourist trade was important to all of them. She truly couldn't anticipate how they would all vote.

Abby also didn't know how Hugo would react to a request to step down as Curator. She could only hope he refused, but she decided not to let herself worry about it until it happened.

If it happened at all.

Abby was learning all over again that appearances could be deceiving. Howard Barnaby had been fooling the residents of Sparrow Island long enough.

THAT EVENING, the Sparrow Island Book Club convened at the library for another special meeting. As vice president and now the acting president, given Janet's resignation, William Jansen called the meeting to order and asked each committee to give a progress report for their fundraiser.

"I guess I can go first," William said. "The publicity committee's spreading the word about the talent show. There will be another article about it in *The Birdcall* this week, as well as a separate color flyer inserted in each paper."

Naomi beamed up at him. "You're doing such a wonderful job of creating a buzz for this event. I just want to thank you for your dedication."

William humbly shrugged off the compliment. "That's just one of the perks of owning your own newspaper. As editor-in-chief, I get to choose the content. So this week I choose to write extensively about the upcoming talent show."

"The tickets are going like hotcakes," Naomi added, giving her committee report. "I won't be at all surprised if we sell out."

The group erupted in spontaneous applause. Then Mary looked around the circle. "Can we get a report from the refreshment committee?"

"Our audience will be well fed," Sandy chimed. "We've got several people volunteering to bring a dessert for the reception after the show."

"And the talent committee?" Mary asked.

Abby and Margaret exchanged glances. They'd met briefly before the meeting to discuss their progress. "We've filled all the slots we need for performers," Margaret announced. "I think the audience is going to be very pleased with the wide variety of talents showcased in our community."

"We're going to ask all the performers to be at the Community Center three hours before the show," Abby added. "I know that seems early, but we want to get a good jump on doing their hair and makeup. That will also give us a chance to work out any wrinkles in the program ahead of time."

Mary smiled. "It sounds like this talent show is all coming together quite nicely. I'm sure there will be some unexpected developments, but communication is the key. As long as we keep in touch with each other, this fundraiser should be a big success."

They spent another hour discussing the talent show, then broke for refreshments. Abby found herself in line between Edmonia and Sandy, who couldn't resist talking about next month's book.

"I was surprised at how much I enjoyed it," Edmonia said, placing a pumpkin bar on her plate. "I've always liked Jane Austen, but this story really spoke to me."

"Her writing is amazing," Sandy concurred. "But the heroine seemed too passive for my taste. She let the hero walk all
over her just because of her guilt for having refused his marriage proposal years before."

The more Abby listened, the more anxious she became to
start the book. There was nothing she liked better than a good,
in-depth book discussion.

"Don't you think that's what makes Austen so fascinating?"
Edmonia poured herself a glass of iced tea. "There's more than
the heroine's guilt issues happening here. There are class issues
and the shallowness of her family. The heroine is battling
between the divided loyalties she feels for her one true love and
her indifferent family."

"I just liked the story." Naomi said, as she moved in line
beside them. "The heroine never stopped loving the hero, even
when it looked as if he was courting another woman right in
front of her."

"He *was* courting another woman right in front of her."
Sandy reached for a napkin. "That was the whole point. He
wanted to make her regret what she'd given up. He had no idea
how much she already regretted it. That was the theme of
the story for me—loyalty. It's reflected in the dynamics of the
family and Anne's relationship with the hero and with her
friends."

"No, I believe it's much simpler than that," Edmonia
exclaimed. "This story's about love. A once-in-a-lifetime, forever kind of love. All that matters is that the hero and heroine
come together in the end."

Naomi laughed. "Spoken like a true romantic."

"I am a romantic," Edmonia admitted. Then she held out
her left hand, her excitement tenable. "I'm also engaged."

Abby gaped at the engagement ring she saw on Edmonia's finger, much too shocked to speak for a moment. The rest of the group gathered around her, *oohing* and *ahhing* over the engagement ring. It was a small, square-cut diamond exquisitely set in a plain platinum band.

"So who's the lucky man?" William asked her.

Edmonia sucked in a deep breath, atwitter with excitement. "His name is Roman Dietz. It's been a whirlwind romance, but I'm in love."

"Well, he's obviously in love with you," Margaret proclaimed, "if he popped the question this fast."

"You're all invited to the wedding," Edmonia announced. "We haven't set a date yet, but something tells me it won't be too far into the future."

Apprehension trickled inside of Abby. She feared Edmonia didn't know Roman Dietz well enough or long enough to make that kind of commitment. It wasn't Abby's place to judge her, but she couldn't help fearing her friend was making a big mistake.

Abby waited for the other well-wishers to disperse before she offered her congratulations.

"I wish you all the best," Abby said. "I hope you'll be very happy."

"I'm sure I will be," Edmonia told her. "I just can't believe this is all happening so fast. My head's still spinning!"

"You had no idea he was going to propose?"

"None!" Edmonia held out her hand to admire her ring. "One minute we were discussing the Nesselrode pudding he'd made for dessert tonight and the next minute he was down on one knee in front of me holding out the ring. I thought I was dreaming."

Abby just hoped Edmonia's dream didn't turn into a nightmare. She had no proof that Roman was the con man, but she didn't want to see her friend walk into a potentially bad situation.

"I just can't believe this is happening," Edmonia said. "Life can change so fast."

She sounded a little wistful and Abby wondered if she regretted moving so hastily. "Are you sure this is what you want, Edmonia?"

The woman looked up at her, uncertainty in her eyes. Then she squared her shoulders. "Positive. I'm tired of playing it safe, Abby. That's gotten me nowhere. This time I'm *not* going to look before I leap."

Those words were still ringing in Abby's ears when she returned home that evening. She followed her sister into the house, not realizing how late it was until she looked at the clock.

"I'm going to bed," Mary said, as soon as her wheelchair crossed over the threshold. Finnegan stood beside her, emitting a loud yawn. "We're both exhausted."

Abby locked the front door behind her. "You're doing a great job as director, Mary. It looks like the talent show's going to be a big hit."

"There's still a lot of work to do," her sister said with a weary sigh. "I wish Janet was around to help me."

Abby wished the same. Margaret had confided in her after the book club meeting that she'd followed Mary's advice and sent Janet a letter of apology. But she hadn't heard back from her and assumed that Janet wasn't yet ready to forgive and forget.

"You know you can ask me if you need anything." Abby told her.

"I do," Mary said with a smile. "Although you have your

hands full with the exhibit opening and your search for Howard Barnaby. Any luck on that front?"

Abby shook her head. "Not so far. The problem is that I'm not sure where to look. I've narrowed down my list of suspects, but unless a vital clue turns up sometime soon, I can't accuse anyone on just my suspicions. That would make me no better than Gary Diggs."

"You'll figure it out," Mary said, completely confident in her sister's abilities. "I'm headed off for bed. Will you get the lights?"

"Yes," Abby replied. "I'm going to stay up and read for a while anyway."

"All right. I'll see you in the morning."

"Goodnight." Abby watched her sister disappear into her bedroom. Then she retrieved Hugo's journal from her bag and carried it into the living room.

Abby chose a seat on the sofa rather than dislodging Blossom, the white, long-haired Persian cat, from her favorite perch on top of the wing chair.

Leafing through the pages of the journal, Abby turned to the significant date in Hugo's journal. The day he met Vanessa Ellsworth.

Everything is going well. It's a cold, blustery day here in Massachusetts. How I miss the warm springs Clarissa and I spent in India. I can still smell the jasmine when I close my eyes. But the East Coast has its positive attributes too.

I attended a wonderful art exhibit last night. I introduced myself to Vanessa Ellsworth and she agreed to have dinner with me tonight. Clarissa wouldn't recognize the old friend from her childhood. We had a spirited debate on the environmental impact of urban sprawl. She is a lovely woman and seems eager to hear about my plan. Clarissa always said I had a way with words . . .

Abby lowered the journal, amazed at how the context of the passage changed when read in its entirety. Gary Diggs had been trying to do more than influence her opinion. He had purposely set out to mislead her.

She wondered if the Ellsworth family knew about Gary's unethical methods and his penchant for cherry-picking information.

Turning to the next passage, Abby was not surprised to find another benign entry. Just like before, Gary had chosen certain sentences that made Hugo seem like a devious scam artist.

I've stayed here long enough. This vacation had been good for me, but now I'm fully renewed and bursting with new ideas. It's the perfect time to return to Sparrow Island before my absence begins to raise suspicions that I'm not interested in my job anymore.

I promised Vanessa that I would continue to raise funds for the conservation project. I can continue my work there just as well, perhaps even more effectively. I promised Vanessa that I'd write to her often. She wants to be updated on my progress.

Abby closed the journal, not needing to read anymore. Hugo's honor and integrity reverberated through every word he wrote. Any remaining doubts she might have had had evaporated.

Hugo wasn't a con man. Just the opposite, in fact. He gave money away instead of hoarding it for himself. He was a servant of God, living his faith, just like the Bible proscribed.

"No one can serve two masters. Either he will hate the one and love the other, or he will be devoted to the one and despise the other. You cannot serve both God and Money" (Matthew 6:24).

Suddenly it dawned on Abby that there had to be an ulterior motive behind Gary Diggs' journey to Sparrow Island. His quest for justice had obviously led him to lie and steal. He'd most likely slashed her tire as well, though Abby had no proof. All she had at this point were her instincts and they told her that Gary Diggs couldn't be trusted.

CHAPTER ✾ SEVENTEEN

B Y FRIDAY, ABBY'S ADRENALINE was running high. She'd spent the week investigating Gary Diggs, and the little information she'd discovered about him convinced her that he himself was up to something fishy. She'd also finished preparing for the exhibit. Now her big night had finally arrived.

She stood at the entrance of The Nature Museum, greeting the formally attired guests as a canopy of stars twinkled high above her. It seemed everyone on Sparrow Island was attending the big event.

Except for one person: Hugo Baron.

Abby kept glancing toward the parking lot, hoping he'd show up soon. He was already an hour late. She kept checking her cell phone and the conservatory's answering machine, but so far he hadn't called.

Where could he be?

Abby had heard more than a few curious whispers already about his absence. As the Curator, Hugo was expected to be here. The fact that he was a no-show only served to fuel all the rumors about him.

"Abby, you look so lovely tonight," Ellen Stanton said as she and George approached the building.

"Thanks, Mom," she replied, reaching out to give her a hug. Her mother looked quite lovely herself, wearing an ivory gown with a peach-colored jacket over it and a strand of pearls around her neck.

"And you look quite dashing," she told her father, admiring his tuxedo with its matching peach silk tie and cummerbund.

"It's not every night I get to take your mother out on the town," he said with a mischievous gleam in his eyes. "I might even talk her into giving me a kiss under the stars."

"Oh, stop it," Ellen scolded, though a pretty pink blush suffused her cheeks.

"This is a big night for you, Abby," her father said, looking around at all the guests. "Looks like you're going to have a great turnout."

"I hope everyone enjoys the exhibit." Now that the time had finally arrived, Abby found herself feeling nervous about it. She'd made little changes to the display all day long just to keep herself busy.

"I'm sure we'll all love it," Ellen proclaimed. "Is your sister here yet?"

She nodded. "Yes, Mary arrived a few minutes ago. She's inside with Henry."

Abby turned to greet the next arriving guest as the Stantons entered the building. Then she glanced once again at the parking lot.

Still no sign of Hugo.

That was strange. She couldn't imagine that he'd forgotten about it or wouldn't call if he was too sick to attend.

"Hello, Abby," Anne Riley greeted her as she arrived on the arm of her husband. Anne wore a full length gown of sparkling silver beads and a matching tiara. "We can't wait . . ."

". . . to see the exhibit." Paul reached out to shake her hand.

"I hope you like it," Abby replied. "It opened my eyes to how the change of season affects so much on Sparrow Island."

"That's what counts," Paul affirmed, "Anne and I don't consider a book a success unless . . ."

". . . we learn something along the way too." Anne tugged on her husband's arm. "Come on, dear, let's go take a look at the exhibit."

Abby watched them enter the building, smiling to herself as the affectionate couple conversed with each other in incomplete sentences. They'd found the perfect match in each other, that much was obvious.

After the last of the guests had arrived, Abby mingled for a while, explaining some of the concepts behind the Rites of Spring exhibit. One of the guests, a young geology professor from UCLA who was vacationing in Green Harbor, engaged her in a fascinating discussion about the formation of the San Juan Islands.

Abby spent the rest of the evening accepting the many compliments for her display, as well as for the lovely dress Mary had purchased for her.

The new shoes pinched her feet a bit, but it was worth it to hear all the rave reviews about the display, including one by the arts and culture reporter from the *Seattle Post* who had traveled by ferry just to see it.

Abby was flushed with success by the time she retreated to

her office to make a phone call to Hugo's house to check on him. She just couldn't understand why he wasn't here to share in their triumph.

She let the telephone ring ten times before finally hanging up. Abby had tried to call his cell phone earlier, but an automated voice told her it was out of the service area. Perhaps Hugo had gone to the mainland to pick up Regina Downey for the opening and gotten held up?

She couldn't think of any other explanation. More than one person had asked her about Hugo's mysterious absence, a few even insinuating that the rumors about his secret identity had kept him away. Abby had staunchly defended him, saying those rumors were based on nothing more than idle speculation.

Only the fact that he wasn't here seemed to prove otherwise.

As she emerged from the hallway, Abby ran into Bobby McDonald. He'd cleaned up nicely for the big event, wearing a dark blue suit and a red tie. His short, dark brown hair was slicked back, taming the cowlick that he usually sported.

"Hey, Abby," he greeted her. "There's a ton of people here and they all really like the exhibit."

"I'm glad to hear it." She smiled as he tugged on his tie. "Is it a little tight?"

"Yeah," he replied. "I tied it myself after I found instructions on how to do it on the Internet. It's harder than it looks."

"I know." Abby remembered watching her father tie the intricate knot in his necktie every Sunday before they went to church. She'd stand with him in front of the long mirror, watching his broad fingers swiftly manipulating the silk fabric.

"There," Bobby said, giving his tie another hard tug. "That's better."

"I think I'll go check on Quackers," Abby said, needing a

break from the crowd. She didn't want to field any more questions about Hugo's absence, especially when she didn't know the reason for it. "Would you like to join me?"

His hazel eyes lit up at the invitation. "I sure would!"

They made their way out of The Nature Museum and headed toward the building that contained her lab. An owl hooted in the distance and Abby could hear the gurgle of the small creek as they walked.

"So where's Hugo tonight?" Bobby asked, repeating the question she'd already heard too many times. "I haven't seen him at all."

"To tell you the truth, Bobby, I don't know where he is. In fact, I'm a little worried about him."

"Maybe he's sick or something."

Abby had considered that possibility, but Hugo had seemed in fine health and spirits when she'd seen him in his office this morning. No, there had to be another reason for his vanishing act.

She just hoped he'd show up soon.

A shadow crossed their path and Abby looked up to see Gary Diggs standing in front of her. He wore a tuxedo like the other guests, but something told her he wasn't out here to compliment her on the exhibit.

"We need to talk," he said briskly.

Abby turned to Bobby, not wanting to expose him to the private investigator's acerbic comments about Hugo. "Why don't you go on ahead and check on Quackers for me. Make sure she's got enough feed and water. I'll catch up with you there in a few minutes, okay?"

"Okay," he agreed, casting a curious glance at Gary before scampering off toward the lab.

When Bobby was gone, she turned back to Gary. "We've got to stop meeting like this," she said wryly. "I'm beginning to think you're stalking me."

It wasn't far from the truth.

She thought about her slashed tire and his sudden appearance on the trail during her hike. Abby wondered what Gary wanted from her this time.

He smiled, though his feral expression didn't put her at ease. "I'm not stalking you, I promise. In fact, I wanted to speak to Mr. Baron tonight, but I can't seem to find him."

"Hugo's not here."

"So I gathered." Gary arched a brow. "Seems rather suspicious, doesn't it? After all, the conservatory is his baby. I can't imagine why he'd skip an event like this with all the potential donors available to schmooze out of their money."

Each time she saw him, Gary Diggs became more and more abrasive. He certainly wasn't anything like the man who had rescued little Adam Halverson, humbly rejecting any type of reward.

Now he seemed to take pleasure in needling her about Hugo. As if mocking her faith in her friend would change her opinion of him. She wondered if the Ellsworths had seen the real Gary Diggs when they'd hired him or if he'd put on a good front, like the first day Abby had met him.

"Hugo isn't like that," she said at last, knowing his comment didn't deserve a response. But Abby couldn't just stand there and let Gary defame her friend.

He shrugged. "It doesn't really matter to me. I can give you the message and let you can pass it on to Hugo when you see him."

"What message?"

Gary took a step closer to her. "I know my investigation has caused somewhat of a disruption in Hugo's life. He's a man of some stature on Sparrow Island, and I'm sure his reputation's very important to him."

Abby waited for him to continue. She could hear the buzz of conversation emanating from the museum, punctuated by bursts of laughter. Everyone seemed to be having a good time at the opening.

Everyone but her.

"The Ellsworth family isn't interested in revenge," Gary continued. "They just want full restitution. If Hugo's willing to provide it to them, then I'll be happy to drop the investigation and return to the mainland."

"You want Hugo to give money to the Ellsworth family."

"I want him to repay the fifty thousand dollars he scammed from Vanessa Ellsworth. I don't think that's too much to ask."

"Fifty thousand dollars? But Hugo isn't Howard Barnaby," Abby said, losing patience with the man. *How many times did she have to say it?* "And he doesn't owe the Ellsworths anything. He only befriended Vanessa in the first place because she was a childhood friend of his late wife's."

"Your defense of your boss is admirable," Gary said in a patronizing tone, "but sadly misguided in this instance. I have solid proof he is Barnaby."

"I don't believe you."

"Proof that I will take to the police," he continued as if she hadn't spoken, "and to the newspapers if Hugo doesn't hand over the fifty thousand dollars in twenty-four hours."

"That's blackmail!"

Gary shook his head. "No, it's simply restitution for the

money the Ellsworth family lost, thanks to Hugo. They're not even charging interest."

Abby didn't know what to say. She was tempted to go to Henry, but not without Hugo's knowledge or permission. Hugo might even think it was worth fifty thousand dollars just to get rid of Gary Diggs and his ugly insinuations about Hugo's past.

"Please just give him my message," Gary told her. "Tell him I'll contact him in twenty-four hours for his answer." Then Gary gave her a jaunty salute and walked away.

Abby stood alone on the path, mulling over Hugo's predicament. Turning down Gary's offer could affect his career and his very livelihood if people in the community wanted him to step down as Curator until he was cleared of all the accusations against him.

Yet, if Hugo gave in to Gary's demand, it would look like an admission of guilt. There was no easy answer. She couldn't even imagine what Hugo's reaction would be when she saw him again.

If she saw him again.

That unwelcome thought came unbidden. Maybe Hugo had tired of the rumors swirling around him and the lack of confidence from some of the community leaders on the town council. But as soon as she considered that possibility, Abby rejected it.

Hugo wasn't the type of man to run away. He didn't shirk his responsibilities either, which meant there was a good reason he wasn't here tonight even if she didn't know it.

Abby had doubted him once. She wasn't going to do it again.

Closing her eyes, she breathed a silent prayer, asking God to give Hugo strength for the days ahead and for herself to provide the support and friendship he needed in his time of trial.

Then she opened her eyes and looked up at the stars. They reminded her that life was full of infinite possibilities.

Her gaze moved to the North Star. Sailors of old had depended on it for navigation in the dark—just like she depended on God to navigate her life.

"Hey," Bobby called out, skipping up the path. "Quackers is doing great. I gave her some more water and checked her cage door to make sure it was locked before I left."

"Thank you, Bobby," she said, grateful for his help. "Shall we head back to the party? Your parents are probably missing you by now."

He sighed. "I suppose. The exhibit's great, but what I'm really excited about is the talent show tomorrow. Wait until you see me juggle."

"I'm excited as well," she told him, though she was feeling a little overwhelmed by everything she had to do.

"It's not very often we have two fun-filled nights in a row on Sparrow Island," Abby continued, her gaze drifting to the parking lot.

There was still no sign of Hugo's car in his reserved spot. She didn't understand how he could miss the opening of an exhibit they'd been planning for months.

"I know," Bobby exclaimed. "This is the best weekend ever!"

Abby wished she could share some of his unbridled enthusiasm, but Gary had just cast a long shadow over her big night. She was worried about Hugo, too, his absence making her somewhat distracted as she mingled with the guests.

Toward the end of the evening, Abby decided to try and call Hugo again. But as she headed for her office, she ran into Edmonia pacing up and down the hallway.

"Edmonia, is something wrong?"

"Oh, Abby," Edmonia cried. "I think I've made a terrible mistake."

CHAPTER ✤ EIGHTEEN

L ET'S GO IN HERE," ABBY said, leading Edmonia into her office. "Please have a seat."

Edmonia sank into the chair. "Oh, Abby, I'm sorry. I didn't mean to take you away from everyone on your big night."

"It's perfectly all right." Abby sat down beside her. "What happened?"

"Roman and I just had our first fight." Edmonia sucked in a deep breath. "It just came out of nowhere. One minute we were laughing and having fun and the next minute—"

The words were cut off by a small sob. Abby handed her a tissue. There was nothing she could say to take away her pain. When the heart loved deeply, it hurt deeply too. All Abby could do at this moment was provide comfort and support.

Edmonia dabbed at her eyes, then gathered herself. "I'm all right."

"Would you like a glass of water?"

Edmonia shook her head. "No, I'm fine. Thank you."

Abby wasn't so sure. There was a slight tremor in Edmonia's voice. "You can stay in here as long as you like."

Edmonia forced a smile. "Is forever too long?"

"You won't want to stay here forever," Abby assured her. "Besides, there are some great appetizers on the refreshment table."

Edmonia's mouth tightened. "That's what our fight was about."

Abby was confused. "You had a fight about the refreshment table?"

"The food *on* the refreshment table." A spark of anger lit her eyes. "I was helping myself to another stuffed mushroom and Roman said ..." Edmonia paused a moment. "And Roman said, *'Are you sure you want that?'* "

Abby blinked, wondering if she'd missed something. "Is that all he said?"

"It may not sound like much to get upset about, but he's been making little pointed comments like that to me all week." She stood up and began to pace across the office. "Helpful advice like: You should wear you hair down more often. It looks nice and helps to cover your wrinkles. Or: It's so nice to be with a woman who doesn't have every guy in the place staring at her."

"Ouch," Abby said aloud, cringing at the backhanded compliment.

"I didn't notice it so much at first," Edmonia mused, "because he just seemed so perfect. But that's the whole problem. He's too perfect and he expects me to be perfect as well."

"You really haven't known him very long," Abby gently reminded her.

"I know." She plopped back in the chair. "And I know I'm probably overreacting too."

Abby wasn't so sure. Roman sounded somewhat controlling to her and those prettily couched comments he'd made to Edmonia had a sharp sting behind them.

"Thank you for listening, Abby. I suppose I'd better go back out there."

"Are you sure?" Abby was tempted to tell Edmonia to dump the guy, but she knew it wasn't her place. Edmonia had to make that decision for herself.

"I don't know," Edmonia replied, making no movement toward the door.

"You know," Abby said, "it always helps me to pray about problems like the one you're having with Roman. Rev. Hale is such a good listener too. You might want to talk to him about all of this—especially before you get married."

Edmonia considered her advice, then nodded. "You're right. I think I will make an appointment to talk with Rev. Hale. I'd be interested in getting a man's point of view on all of this."

Abby walked her to the door. "And just for the record, I've already had four of those stuffed mushrooms myself. They're irresistible."

Edmonia laughed. "They are. And just to show Roman, I think I'll have *two*."

As they walked down the hallway, Abby saw a light shining through the crack of Hugo's closed office door. Relief flowed through her.

"Would you mind going on without me?" Abby asked Edmonia. "I need to talk to Hugo for a moment."

"Sure," she replied. "I didn't realize he was here. Some

people were saying . . ." her voice trailed off, then she smiled. "Never mind."

Edmonia continued down the hallway, looking better than she had a few moments ago. Abby saw Roman meet her at the refreshment table and give her a big hug.

While Abby was glad to see Edmonia happier, she hoped the woman followed through on her plan to pray and talk with Rev. Hale.

Abby turned toward Hugo's office, knocking on the door at the same time as she opened it. "I've been wondering where you've . . ."

Her voice trailed off when she saw Wallace Sibley rifling through Hugo's desk. He looked up at her entrance, his face going pale.

"Hello, Dr. Stanton."

"What are you doing in here?"

Wallace wore his standard uniform of navy blue coveralls and a blue pinstriped painter's cap. A uniform that granted him easy access to every room in the building, along with his set of keys. Now Abby knew why so much dust had been accumulating in her office. Wallace was too busy snooping to clean.

"Well?" she pressed. "Why are you in Hugo's office?"

"I'm just . . . doing my job," he sputtered, straightening the papers in front of him. "You know . . . cleaning up around the place."

He wasn't a very good liar.

"Wallace, we both know you are *not* cleaning. What are you looking for in that desk?"

He hesitated, eyeing the door. She moved in front of it to

prevent his escape. Abby didn't intend to let him go until he told her the truth.

"Look, let's just pretend you never saw me in here, okay?" Wallace took a step toward her. "I'm not here to cause any trouble for you."

"Are you here to cause trouble for Hugo?"

He folded his arms across his chest. "I'm just looking for the truth."

Wallace's demeanor wasn't that of the mild-mannered care-taker that she'd come to know in the last couple of weeks.

She moved toward the door. "Perhaps you'd be more comfortable talking to Sheriff Cobb. I'm sure he's still here."

"Wait," Wallace cried, his bravado crumpling. "I'm not doing anything criminal. I'm just looking for a story."

"A story," she echoed, as confused by his answer as she was by his behavior.

He hesitated, then shrugged his narrow shoulders. "I suppose it's going to come out soon enough, so I might as well tell you. Regina Downey, also known as the famous movie star Regina Wilder, is going to marry Hugo Baron. That will make husband number nine for her."

Abby's head was spinning. "What are you talking about?"

"I'm a reporter for the *Daily Scoop*," he explained. "I just took this gig to try to find some juicy details about the happy couple."

The *Daily Scoop* was a cheap tabloid published in California. The focus of its articles was on the private lives of movie stars, the juicier the better.

"Even at Regina's age she's still big news," Wallace continued. "And I'm about to scoop everyone in the industry with the exclusive of her impending nuptials."

"So you're a reporter?"

"I've been working undercover." Wallace acknowledged, then shook his head in disdain. "And I have to say this is one of the toughest assignments I've ever taken. You people actually expected me to work around here."

In her search for the elusive Howard Barnaby, she'd let another imposter play out a masquerade right under her nose. "Wallace, you're fired."

He smiled. "Fine with me. I didn't want to clean up after this shindig anyway. Besides, there's no good dirt here, and I'm talking about some good gossip, not the dirt the tourists track in here every day. I guess I'll have to get the goods on Hugo and Regina someplace else."

Abby held out her hand. "I'll take your keys before you leave."

Wallace dug into the pocket of his coveralls, then pulled out the ring of keys that opened every building on the conservatory.

Then another possibility hit her. "Are you the one who vandalized the exhibit?"

He reared back, taking offense at her words. "Of course not. I didn't come here to sabotage your exhibit. All that did was delay my big scoop when the opening was postponed." He scowled. "I thought for sure Hugo would bring Regina here as his date tonight."

"You're going to be waiting a lot longer for that big scoop than you think," Abby told him as she escorted him out of the office.

"I don't think so," Wallace countered. "I smell a story. There's definitely something fishy going on with Hugo and Regina."

"The only thing fishy around here is your ethics as a journalist," Abby replied. "I intend to call your editor on Monday morning and make a complaint."

He grinned at the threat. "Go right ahead and call him. My editor is the one who sent me here undercover in the first place." Then he tipped his hat to her. "Good-bye, Dr. Stanton. Believe it or not, it was a real pleasure to meet you. I've never met anyone who knows as much about birds as you do."

Abby shook her head as he left the museum. The guests were thinning out; only a few stragglers were left now, including her parents.

"It was a wonderful party," Ellen exclaimed, her eyes shining with delight. "I'm so proud of you."

"Thanks, Mom," she replied, looking around the room. There was still no sign of Hugo. Even if he did show up now, he'd missed the exhibit opening. Disappointment seeped through her.

"Is something wrong?" George asked her, reaching out to rub her shoulder. "You look upset."

She swallowed a sigh. "I'm just concerned about Hugo. I don't understand why he's not here tonight."

"That isn't like him," George concurred. "I hope he's all right."

"So do I," Abby replied. "I also hope he's prepared for the message Gary Diggs wants me to give to him."

"What message is that?" her father asked.

Abby waited until Wilma walked outside with the rest of the guests, then she turned back to her parents. "He's giving Hugo twenty-four hours to hand over fifty thousand dollars as restitution for the money Howard Barnaby took from Vanessa Ellsworth."

"And if he doesn't?"

"Then he's going to the police to have Hugo arrested."

"He can't do that," Ellen exclaimed. "Hugo isn't Howard Barnaby."

"That's what I've tried to tell him," Abby said, "over and over again. He just won't listen."

George rubbed his chin, then looked at his daughter. "What do you think Hugo will do?"

"I honestly don't know," Abby replied. "All I do know is that he can't keep living under this cloud of suspicion that Gary Diggs has created."

The concern she saw on her parents' faces matched her own. Gary wasn't giving Hugo a choice, he was making an ultimatum. It was a threat to destroy Hugo's reputation if he didn't hand over a large chunk of cash.

"I think Hugo should tell Henry about it," George said at last. "That kind of deal may not even be legal."

"I agree," Abby said. "But that's Hugo's call to make. I just hope he shows up here soon so I can tell him what's happening. If he hasn't returned by tomorrow night, I don't know what Gary Diggs will do."

"Oh, I'm sure Hugo will be back before then," Ellen said. "He's performing in the talent show, after all."

Abby wished she could be as confident. Hugo's primary responsibility was to the conservatory. Since he hadn't shown up for the opening, she had no reason to believe he'd make it to the talent show either.

"Don't give up on him," George admonished her, as if he were able to read her thoughts. "There's a reason Hugo isn't here tonight. And I'm sure it's a good reason."

Abby nodded, then she walked her parents out the door.

It was getting late and she was having trouble holding back a yawn.

After they left, she locked up The Nature Museum for the night, telling herself she'd clean up the mess in the morning. With Wallace no longer working here, she'd have to recruit some help to get the job done in time to make it to the talent show. At least she knew she could always count on Bobby to volunteer.

Abby walked down the hallway, then stood in the doorway of Hugo's office. It looked so empty without him. She walked inside, then straightened the pile of papers Wallace had been rummaging through when she'd caught him in here.

Taking a seat behind Hugo's desk, Abby leaned back and thought about everything that had been happening on Sparrow Island lately. The petty thefts. The vandalism of the Rites of Spring exhibit. The dogged determination of Gary Diggs to prove that Hugo was a con man. Her search for the real Howard Barnaby.

As events and conversations drifted through her mind, Abby wondered if she'd been making this case too complicated. Maybe she'd been looking for Howard Barnaby in all the wrong places.

What if he wasn't really the villain that Gary Diggs had made him out to be?

There was only one way to find out.

CHAPTER ✿ NINETEEN

Hugo was still missing. Abby stood backstage at the talent show on Saturday evening, trying to keep track of her performers and keep her mind off of Hugo. She hadn't seen or heard from him since Friday morning.

Her concern was turning to panic, especially since he was scheduled to perform in less than an hour. Her father had stopped by Hugo's house earlier in the day, but there had been no sign of him anywhere.

It was as if he'd vanished into thin air. No one she'd talked to had seen or heard from him. Abby was tempted to go on her own search-and-rescue mission, but she had no idea where to look.

Soon Gary Diggs would show up, demanding his money. Abby supposed she could try to stall him until Hugo finally arrived, but she didn't know when that would be. Gary didn't strike her as a patient man. He'd pushed his theory that Hugo was Howard Barnaby without even taking the time to investigate any other suspects.

But none of that mattered now.

"Okay, let's take a role call," Abby shouted out to her group of performers.

Each book club member had been assigned a particular duty for the night of the talent show. Sandy was in charge of staffing the refreshment table. Margaret was taking tickets at the door. Naomi was in charge of running the lights and the recorded music.

Abby's job consisted of organizing all the performers and making certain that they appeared onstage and in the correct order.

William walked by her, performing vocal exercises. He'd been recruited at the last minute to emcee the event. Rev. Hale had been the book club's first choice, but he'd been called away to the bedside of a sick congregation member.

Now the newspaper man kept pacing the floor backstage and rehearsing his opening joke. Abby was empathetic, knowing she'd be nervous, as well, speaking in front of such a large crowd.

"Are Warren and Mercedes Meyers here?" Abby called out.

"Yes, we're right here," Warren replied, shepherding his daughter toward Abby. The two of them planned to perform a tap dance routine to a special rendition of "Me and My Shadow." "I think we're ready to go, aren't we, Mercedes?"

His seventeen-year-old daughter looked less than enthusiastic. "I guess."

"Great," Abby replied, then she looked at the next name on her list. "Mrs. Mulligan?"

No one responded. Abby looked around the backstage area in alarm. Father Timothy's housekeeper was performing an Irish step dance. If both she and Hugo were absent, the talent show wouldn't even last an hour.

"Here I am," Mrs. Mulligan cried, patting her short curls. "Edmonia was just putting the finishing touches on my hair."

Though Abby hadn't had a chance to talk to Edmonia, the hairdresser seemed fully recovered from her first fight with Roman. Abby had been hearing her melodic laugh ever since she'd arrived at the Community Center over three hours ago.

"Al Minsky?" Abby called out, looking for her mechanic among the bustle of people backstage. "Al, are you here?"

"I'm right in front of you."

She stared at the distinguished looking man standing before her, then blinked, realizing it really was Al Minsky.

He wore a black suit and a crisp white shirt with a silver gray cravat. The violin cradled in his broad hands was polished to a high sheen.

"I'm sorry, Al," Abby said, shocked by his transformation. "I guess I didn't see you there."

She marked his name on the list, then moved to the one directly below it. "Bobby McDonald?"

"Present and ready to juggle," Bobby announced. He carried a carton of eggs with him, making Abby hope they had a mop handy.

"Don't worry." Bobby smiled when he saw her expression. "I hard-boiled them last night, then dyed them with bright colors so they'd be easier for the audience to see."

"Good idea," Abby replied, smoothing one hand over his wayward hair.

Mary moved through the crowd in her wheelchair. "Five minutes until showtime everyone. This is your five-minute warning."

Abby stepped toward her sister and asked in a low voice, "Have you seen any sign of Hugo?"

"Not yet," Mary replied. "I'll keep a lookout for him."

"Thanks." Abby's attention returned to her list. "Paul and Anne Riley?" She looked up from the paper. "Are the Rileys here?"

Graves, the Rileys' butler, appeared out of nowhere. "They're here, but they don't have their traditional Japanese costumes on yet. It may take them a few minutes to dress."

"No hurry," Abby assured him. "Their Kabuki dance is near the end of the program, so they have some time to get ready yet."

"I'll make certain they're prepared to go onstage," Graves promised her before disappearing again.

Hugo was scheduled as the last performer for the evening, though it was beginning to look as if he wouldn't perform at all.

"Two minutes to showtime," Mary announced, making another pass through the backstage crowd. "Showtime in two minutes."

Abby hurried through the rest of her list, then placed Warren and Mercedes next to their entrance point on the edge of the stage. William Jansen stood near them, clearing his throat and checking his appearance in a small mirror hung on the wall.

"I'm a little nervous about this," Mercedes admitted to her father, her freckles standing out on her pale face. Her blonde hair had been swept up into a classic French twist which was quite flattering on her.

Warren placed both hands on his daughter's thin shoulders and gave them a comforting squeeze. "No reason to be nervous, hon. We're in this together."

The lights went down in the room, signaling the start of the show.

"Okay, William," Abby prodded the emcee, "that's your cue."

He took a deep breath, then headed out onto the stage. Abby watched from the sidelines as he began his opening monologue, drawing laughs and applause from the overflow crowd.

"Okay, you're on," Abby told the Meyers act.

Warren peeked past the curtain and into the crowd. "Wow. There are a lot of people out there."

"Come on, Dad," Mercedes said, grabbing her father's hand. "Let's do this thing."

Abby watched them take the stage as silence descended over the audience. A moment later, the first strains of their song began, followed by their choreographed tap routine.

Mary moved up beside her. "You'll never guess who's here!"

"Hugo?" Abby exclaimed, relief flooding her.

"No," Mary said hastily. "It's Janet. I just saw her in the audience. I called her yesterday and asked her to come. She didn't give me an answer either way, but I'm so happy to see her here tonight."

Abby smiled, trying to hide her disappointment that it wasn't Hugo. "That's wonderful."

Mary reached for her hand, giving it a reassuring squeeze. "He'll be here."

Four more acts performed after the Meyers, with Al Minsky drawing cries for an encore after his moving violin performance. He obliged the crowd with two more songs, buying Hugo some extra time.

Then Bobby took the stage. Abby held her breath as he tossed three eggs into the air simultaneously and began to juggle. A catch behind his back drew a loud gasp from the crowd, then wild applause as he concluded his juggling finale.

Bobby exited the stage, his cheeks flushed with his success.

"You were incredible," Abby exclaimed. "You didn't drop one egg."

"I know!" Bobby couldn't stop grinning. "I'm a real juggler!"

"You certainly are." Abby scanned her list, realizing that only the Rileys and Hugo were left to perform. The evening was flying by and the talent show seemed to be a hit with everyone.

Paul and Anne finally made an appearance dressed in authentic Japanese costumes. Abby was barely able to recognize the couple in their wigs and full stage makeup. The stunning orange kimono Anne wore was embroidered with bright yellow thread. Paul's robe was a fiery red, adorned with blue dragons.

"As soon as you hear your music begin," Abby told them, "you can go onstage."

The couple smiled at each other, then joined hands as they prepared to walk out to perform for the large audience.

Edmonia appeared at Abby's side. "This is so much fun. I think our book club should put on a talent show every year."

"Maybe we should wait a month or two before we bring it up for a vote," Abby recommended. "Just to give everyone a chance to recover."

Edmonia laughed. "Smart plan."

"You're in a good mood," Abby observed "I take it you've worked things out with Roman?"

"I have." Edmonia turned to face her. "I broke off the engagement this afternoon."

Abby didn't know what to say. Edmonia did not act like a woman who had just lost her fiancé. Then again, what better indication that the two of them weren't right for each other?

"It was for the best," Edmonia continued. "After I talked with Rev. Hale this morning, I realized I was tolerating Roman's cruel remarks just to avoid loneliness. I deserve better than that."

"You do," Abby confirmed. "We all do. But I have to say I'm surprised that you're taking it so well."

"Why waste time mourning over a guy like him?" Edmonia grinned. "Spring's a time for new beginnings and I'm ready to enjoy every moment of it."

The sound of applause made Abby's heart skip a beat. The Kabuki dance was over and Hugo still hadn't made an appearance. Her disappointment cut deep as she went in search of William.

"Have you seen our emcee?" Abby asked her sister. "He needs to announce that the show is over."

Mary frowned. "Hugo never showed up?"

Abby shook her head. "I'm really starting to worry about him now. This just isn't like Hugo at all. As soon as the lights go back on I'm going to find Henry and ask him about filing a missing person report."

"Good idea," Mary replied, then moved her wheelchair closer to Abby, "but the show's not over yet."

"What do you mean?"

Mary took a deep breath. "I'm going to perform."

Abby stared at her sister, amazed that she'd made such a decision at the last moment. "Are you sure about this?"

Mary hesitated a moment, then nodded. "I'm positive." She reached into the bag attached to her wheelchair and pulled out some sheet music. "Can you give this to the accompanist?"

"Of course." Abby looked at the crude musical notations written in pencil on the paper. "Did you write this song?"

"No," Mary replied, rolling her wheelchair toward the stage. "But I know who did."

While Abby gave the sheet music to the piano accompanist, she kept one eye on her sister. Stage fright could still strike

Mary at any moment and Abby wanted to be ready to assist
her if it did.

Mary moved to the center of the stage and lowered the
microphone to her level. She looked out into the crowd, her
face as white as the crepe blouse she wore. But she didn't back
down. Instead, she began to speak.

"I'd like to dedicate this song to two of my best friends,
Janet Heinz and Margaret Blackstock. They wrote it about ten
years ago and performed it together at my birthday party. Now
I'd like to return the favor."

Silence descended over the crowd as the first piano notes
sounded in the auditorium.

Abby clenched her hands together, praying that Mary could
beat the stage fright that had plagued her since she was a
teenager.

But Mary didn't even hesitate. Instead, she smiled and
began to sing in her clear, sweet voice.

> *I can count on you*
> *Whenever I'm feelin' blue*
> *Day or night, wrong or right,*
> *We'll be friends, through and through*
> *I can always count on you . . .*

Tears pricked Abby's eyes as she watched her sister's flawless
performance. Her voice never wavered and her gaze was fixed
on the two women in the audience who hadn't spoken to each
other in two weeks.

When the song ended, the audience began to applaud and
shout for an encore. Then Mary held up her hands for silence.

"At this time," she said into the microphone, "I'd like to invite the composers of this song onstage to sing it with me."

Abby's breath caught in her throat, aware this request could backfire on her sister. Janet and Margaret could get up and leave the Community Center, just like they'd left the restaurant two weeks ago.

But to her amazement, Abby saw Janet rise out of her chair and walk toward the stage. Margaret joined her at the stairs. They looked at each other for a moment, then climbed up onto the stage together.

"Ready, girls?" Mary asked, as they stood on either side of her. She motioned for the accompanist to begin playing the song again.

Their voices were soft and hesitant at first, then they grew stronger. By the last verse, they were all grinning and entwined arm-in-arm.

Abby wiped away tears of joy as she began to applaud with the rest of the crowd. Mary had overcome her fear of the stage by focusing not on herself but on the two friends who meant so much to her.

The crowd was still cheering as the three women onstage began to sing another song a cappella.

"Looks like I missed a great show."

Abby turned around to find the man who was trying to destroy Hugo standing right behind her.

Gary Diggs had arrived for his answer.

CHAPTER ✿ TWENTY

THE SHOW ISN'T OVER YET," Abby replied, "and neither is the twenty-fours you gave Hugo."

Gary checked his watch. "It's close enough by my estimation. So where is he?"

Abby wasn't going to lie to him. "I don't know."

Mary, Janet and Margaret exited the stage, laughing and crying at the same time. As the crowd dispersed for refreshments, several people gathered around the trio to congratulate them on their performance and rave about the talent show in general.

Abby did not want anyone overhearing Gary's cutting comments about Hugo, so she motioned him to join her by the costume cupboard where there were far fewer people milling about.

"These delay tactics aren't going to work," Gary said, following behind her. "I can go to the newspapers right now and give them enough ammunition against Hugo, or should I say Howard Barnaby, for the authorities to hound him for years."

"You think so?"

Gary Diggs didn't scare her anymore. In truth, he'd never scared her. Abby realized now that it was her own doubts about her friend that had frightened her more than any baseless accusations a stranger could make.

Thankfully, those doubts had disappeared, making her friendship with Hugo even stronger than before. They'd come through the storm together and now she was ready to enjoy the sunshine. Ready to shine a bright light on everything about this case.

If Abby had her way, Gary Diggs would never bother Hugo again.

Gary sized her up, losing some of his bravado. "Look, I'll give Hugo until midnight tonight to come up with an answer. He either gives me fifty thousand dollars to make this whole thing go away or I go to the police and the newspapers with my proof that he's Howard Barnaby."

Before Abby could reply, Hugo appeared from the other side of the costume cupboard.

"I can give you an answer right now," Hugo told him, moving to stand right beside Abby. "And that answer is no."

She'd never been so happy to see someone in her life. Hugo looked healthy and hearty, relieving her fears that some illness or injury had kept him away.

They stood together now, presenting a united front against Gary's assault on Hugo's reputation and the future of the conservatory.

Gary looked taken aback by Hugo's response to his blackmail. "Did you hear what I said? I'll go to the police—and to every tabloid I can find who will listen to your sordid story. By the time I'm through, your life and your reputation will be in shreds."

Hugo smiled. "I'm not intimidated by your threats, Mr. Diggs." Then he quoted from the bible:

"The Lord is with me, I will not be afraid. What can man do to me?" (Psalm 118:6)

"You should be afraid," Gary countered, his eyes shifting nervously back and forth. "I've got the goods on you. For one thing, I know that you attended Oxford in England. I've also recently discovered that Howard Barnaby isn't your real full name, either."

"You're right," Hugo said. "Howard Barnaby isn't my real name. It never was."

"You know what I mean." Gary narrowed his eyes. "Howard is your middle name and Barnaby is your mother's maiden name. I notice you've never gone by your first name at all, though that's hardly surprising, since most men are ashamed to be called by a girl's name."

Gary's dig about a feminine first name niggled something in Abby's brain. Before she could cultivate it, the man continued his rant.

"And don't deny that you were at Oxford," Gary said, "I've seen the records."

"You're right," Hugo replied, not looking the least bit ruffled by this latest accusation. "I did spend a semester at Oxford. That was over thirty years ago and I was married at the time and living in a small cottage just off campus with my wife."

"Aha," Gary exclaimed, stabbing a finger in his direction, "so you admit it!"

"I admit I was at Oxford," Hugo said, "but so were thousands of other students. You can play the innuendo game all day long, Gary. You still can't prove that I'm Howard Barnaby."

Abby saw her opportunity and took it. "But I can prove you're not a private investigator for the Ellsworth family."

"What?" Gary gaped at her. "You're crazy."

"Actually, I'm sorry I didn't go to the source sooner. You see, Mr. Diggs, I just naturally trust people. When you told me you worked for the Ellsworth family, I believed you."

Hugo turned to her, bewilderment clouding his blue eyes. "Are you saying that he *doesn't* work for the Ellsworth family?"

"Not anymore." Abby folded her arms across her chest, enjoying the moment. "He did work for them for a few short months, but as a gardener, not a private investigator. That's when he overheard stories about the con man who scammed Vanessa Ellsworth out of more than fifty thousand dollars."

A flush of indignation crawled up Gary's face. "My official job title with the Ellsworth family really doesn't matter. I know Hugo is Howard Barnaby and I know he took that money from Vanessa. I found the proof in a box of old letters."

Abby turned to Hugo, no longer interested in convincing Gary of anything. "He'd heard about Howard Barnaby's con job and the time period it happened—the same time period when you met her. When I called the Ellsworth family this morning, they told me they fired Gary after they found him rifling through some old letters belonging to Vanessa that he'd found in her room. They must have been your letters to her. He saw the dates and assumed you were Barnaby."

"Only because that's the logical assumption," Gary retorted.

"He must have tracked you to Sparrow Island and decided to make your life miserable until you agreed to his blackmail to make him go away." Abby could see by the expression on Gary's face that she was right. "I can only assume his efforts to convince me of your guilt were designed to make his offer more attractive."

"Listen," Gary sputtered, angry at being ignored. "The Ellsworth family isn't to be trusted. I'm doing this for . . . for the good of mankind. I'm planning to donate that fifty thousand dollars to charity. So I suggest you hand it over if you know what's good for you."

Sgt. Henry Cobb ambled over to them. "Is that a blackmail threat I hear?"

Abby loved his sense of timing. "Yes. He wants Hugo to pay him fifty thousand dollars in exchange for leaving the island and stopping all the slanderous rumors he's been spreading about him."

"They're not rumors," Gary insisted. "He's Howard Barnaby. He has to be!"

Henry ignored him, turning to Abby. "What do you know about this?"

"Charles Ellsworth, Vanessa's nephew, told me that Howard Barnaby confessed to his crimes five years ago and served a short prison sentence."

Gary shook his head. "No, that can't be true."

Henry looked in his direction. "If it comes to taking Abby's word or your word, Mr. Diggs, I'll take Abby's every time."

His loyalty touched her. "Charles Ellsworth told me something else too," Abby continued. "Howard Barnaby showed real remorse for his crimes and paid restitution, plus interest, to all of his victims.

Henry took a step closer to Gary. "It sounds like we need to take a ride down to the station and have a little chat, Mr. Diggs."

Gary's shoulders sagged. "I want a lawyer."

Henry nodded, then escorted him toward the exit. "I'm sure that can be arranged."

Abby watched them leave, then turned to Hugo, stunned that it was finally over. "I think that's the last we'll see of Gary Diggs. He saw an opportunity to make some easy money and tried to sell you your reputation back. Little did he know you never lost it."

Hugo smiled. "Thanks to friends like you standing by my side. I think that's the one thing Gary never counted on."

"I'm just glad you're here."

He sighed. "I'm so sorry I missed the exhibit opening last night, Abby, and left you to handle it on our own. I assume Wallace gave you my message."

She shook her head. "No. As a matter of fact, I fired him last night when I caught him rifling through your desk."

Hugo's mouth dropped open. "You caught him doing what?"

"It seems Gary Diggs wasn't the only one working under phony pretenses around here. Wallace Sibley is really a tabloid reporter trying to get a big scoop about your romance with Regina Downey."

"My romance with Regina Downey?" he echoed. Then a chuckle started low in his chest and grew until he was booming with laughter.

Several people turned to stare at him as they mingled backstage with the performers.

"Regina Downey is my sister-in-law," Hugo explained at last. "She just underwent surgery for a serious condition and gave me power-of-attorney over her affairs. But she made me promise complete secrecy until it was all over. That's why I couldn't tell you anything about her."

"She's your sister-in-law?" Abby breathed in amazement.

He nodded. "She's my late wife's youngest sister and was the baby of the family. Right before Clarissa passed away, she asked me to watch out for Regina. It's a promise that I intend to keep."

"And Regina was an actress?"

Hugo nodded. "Quite a talented actress too. Unfortunately, Regina's made some poor choices in her personal life and now finds herself alone and distrusting of almost everyone. I'm the only one she believes will not spread any gossip about her life just to make an easy buck."

It saddened Abby to think that others held life so cheaply. People like Wallace and Gary, who found money more important than loving their neighbor.

At least Abby finally understood Hugo's strange behavior of late. All the phone calls from Regina. The unexplained absences where he probably had to travel to the mainland to attend to her legal business while she underwent medical treatment.

"Regina suddenly took a turn for the worst yesterday afternoon," Hugo continued. "That's why I had to miss the opening. She didn't have anyone else to stay by her side."

Abby's heart went out to him. It seemed Hugo had lived up to his responsibility after all, following the Lord's charge to offer comfort to the sick.

"I knew you could handle the exhibit opening on your own," Hugo said, full of confidence in her abilities. "I'm just sorry I missed it."

"So am I," Abby told him. "How's your sister-in-law doing now?"

His face brightened. "Much better. The doctor said she's well on her way to a full recovery. And Regina's hired a wonderful nurse who will take good care of her when she returns home."

"That's wonderful news. I'm sure you must be very relieved."

"I am," he replied. "My prayers were answered. Though I knew whatever the outcome, Regina was safe in God's hands."

As they headed toward the steps leading off the stage, Abby glimpsed the Rileys seated at the make-up station. Graves was hastily trying to remove all the thick white makeup on their faces while they cheerfully chatted about the good times they'd had traveling the world.

That's when it all clicked.

She finally understood why Gary Diggs had come to Sparrow Island to find Howard Barnaby. In his rush to iden-tify the con man and cash in on his jackpot, he'd narrowed his focus on one man.

The wrong man.

Hugo wasn't the prey Gary had sought. But the real Howard Barnaby was living on Sparrow Island. In fact, he was right here in this Community Center.

"I feel like celebrating," Hugo said. "Would you like to join me in some dessert?"

Most of the audience was still milling around the Community Center, enjoying the desserts and punch from the refreshment table and talking about the talent show.

She saw Rick DeBow and Wilma Washburn chatting with each other over a cup of coffee. And there was Mr. Danker, the juggler, congratulating Bobby for his great success onstage.

It looked to Abby like no one had left the Community Center yet, the sign of a great party. And it was just about to get even better.

"Dessert sounds wonderful," Abby agreed, "but first I'd like you to meet some new friends of mine."

She steered him over to the Rileys, then made the introductions. "Paul and Anne, this is Hugo Baron, the Curator of the Sparrow Island Nature Conservatory. Hugo, these are the Rileys, co-authors of some wonderful children's books."

"Nice to meet you," Hugo said.

Then Abby turned to Graves, who was removing the black wig from his sister's head. "And this is the man I've been searching for all these weeks. Hugo, I'd like to introduce you to Mr. Marion Howard Barnaby Graves."

CHAPTER ❧ TWENTY-ONE

ANNE GASPED, HER HAND flying to her mouth.

Graves carefully placed the wig on the table in front of him, his expression betraying nothing. "How did you know?"

"Actually, I didn't put it all together until just a few minutes ago," Abby replied, "when I learned that Howard Barnaby's real first name was most often used for a girl instead of a boy. That's when I remembered your sister calling you Marion the afternoon I came over to the house for tea."

"Oh dear," Anne said, casting a guilty look up at her brother. "I'm so sorry, Marion. I've always had such a big mouth."

"Please don't feel bad," Graves told her, patting her shoulder. "The only reason I was trying to keep my past a secret was to protect you and Paul. Otherwise, it wouldn't matter to me."

Then he looked over at Hugo. "I owe you an apology, sir. I should have stepped forward when I heard the rumors that there was a private investigator on the island looking for a con man named Howard Barnaby."

"Rumors," Paul echoed, a quizzical expression on his face. "What rumors? I haven't heard . . ."

". . . anything about this," Anne continued. Then she looked over at her husband. "Maybe we need to spend a little less time . . ."

". . . in the fictional world," Paul said, "and more time in the real world."

"Don't blame yourselves," Graves told them. "It's all my fault. I have to own up to my mistakes and quit hiding behind the two of you."

Abby could see the pain in his eyes and truly believed he regretted his past actions. She wondered what had made Graves and his sister, both from the same family, turn out so differently.

Anne had a sweet, almost ethereal air about her and a joy that touched everyone she met. Graves, on the other hand, walked around as if a dark cloud always hovered over his head.

"There's no excuse for what I did," Graves continued, his shoulders straight and rigid, "and I brought it all on myself."

"Don't say that," Anne admonished him.

"It's true," he countered, a muscle twitching in his jaw. "I ran away from home when I was a teenager, tired of our parents telling me what to do. I had no idea how tough it really was in the world. I thought I could make my fortune and show them all."

Abby glanced at Hugo, wondering if he could empathize with the man. Like Graves, Hugo had left home at a young age. Both men had faced the world head on with no safety net to catch them if they fell.

Yet, they'd each taken such very different paths. One had turned to deception and crime, while the other had spent a lifetime in pursuit of philanthropic projects and learning.

"Our parents were very hard on him," Anne said softly. "Marion was the oldest of six children and they expected a lot from him.

"And were sadly disappointed in me, I'm afraid." Graves sighed. "Naturally, I didn't make my fortune. I could barely make ends meet to survive. The only thing that saved me were kind people I met along my travels who offered me a place to stay and food to eat."

"There are many good people in this world," Hugo observed. "More than you'd expect by listening to the evening news."

"Yes, there are good people everywhere," Graves agreed. "And I soon learned to take advantage of them."

Paul stood up and grasped his brother-in-law's shoulder. "You don't owe anyone an explanation. You've paid for your crimes."

"No," Graves countered. "I want to get this all out in the open. I should have done it as soon as I heard about the private investigator."

"He would have just blackmailed you too," Hugo said generously. "Gary Diggs wasn't here seeking justice, he just wanted a payout."

"That used to be my only goal in life too," Graves replied. "I learned to play the game very well, but I know now that I can never make up for the pain I caused along the way. It wasn't a game to people who called me their friend."

Abby's heart ached for him and for his victims. She'd recently seen firsthand how loneliness could drive a person to make some foolish choices and hasty decisions. At least Edmonia had come to her senses in time. Too many people didn't discover the error in their thinking until it was too late.

"What made you finally stop?" Hugo asked. "Did you get caught?"

Graves graced them with a rare smile. "In a way I suppose that I did get caught. In a web of my own making. You see, Vanessa Ellsworth was going to be my biggest score ever, but I hadn't counted on falling in love with her."

Anne's eyes misted and she reached for a tissue.

"She constantly talked to me about her faith in God," Graves continued, "and made me see that the world wasn't just a playground built for my own amusement. She taught me that people mattered and that love could fill any void."

"She sounds wonderful," Abby said softly.

Graves swallowed hard. "She was the love of my life. I confessed everything to the police and we were going to be married after I completed my prison sentence. Only, she passed away suddenly while I was incarcerated."

Anne reached for another tissue. "The authorities in Massachusetts wouldn't even let my brother attend Vanessa's funeral."

"It doesn't matter now," Graves said solemnly. "I know she's in a better place."

"So are you," Paul told him. "And we're thrilled to have you living with us."

Graves smiled again. "I'm not sure *thrilled* is the appropriate word. But I intend to work off every penny of the debt I owe you." He turned to Abby. "Paul and Anne loaned me the money to make full restitution to all my victims."

Abby now admired Graves even more for not becoming

bitter at Vanessa's death and returning to his life of crime. Instead, he seemed intent on redeeming himself. Or perhaps proving himself worthy of Vanessa's love.

"It wasn't a loan," Paul countered, "Anne and I . . ."

". . . consider it a gift." Anne smiled up at her brother. "We love you. You don't owe us anything."

At last Abby understood why Graves worked as the Rileys' butler. The odd arrangement allowed him to earn enough money to pay off his debt, especially since it wasn't easy for an ex-convict to find employment.

Yet, he provided something for them too. With Graves around to keep their household in order, the Rileys were free to indulge in their adventures, both fictional and real, anytime they wanted.

"Now don't start that again," Graves told his brother-in-law. "I'm paying you back that money, no matter how long it takes."

"Then I hope it takes a long time," Anne said, "because we love having you around."

"We also love apple pie," Paul chimed, taking the wig off his head. He turned to his wife. "Shall we go grab . . ."

". . . some dessert?" Anne said. "I'd love to."

Graves accompanied his sister and brother-in-law to the refreshment table, leaving Abby and Hugo backstage.

"Do you suppose there will be any apple pie left for us?" Hugo asked her with a twinkle in his eye.

Before she could reply, Mary approached them. "I just heard the news! Everybody's talking about the fact that the private investigator is a fraud and Hugo's name has been cleared."

"Yes," Abby said. "Isn't it wonderful?"

"So wonderful," Mary replied, "that I think it calls for a

special celebration." Then she waved at William, who stood near the stage curtain.

He nodded when he saw her, then walked out onto the stage. William picked up the microphone. "Hello, everyone. May I have your attention, please?"

Abby turned to her sister. "What's going on?"

Mary grinned. "You'll see."

"The Sparrow Island Book Club would like to present a special finale to this evening's talent show," William announced. "If you will all please take your seats, we will resume the show."

Abby looked over at Hugo. "It looks like you may get to perform your birdcalls after all."

"This finale isn't a solo act," Mary said, heading toward the stage. "Come on, you two."

Abby followed her sister, still clueless about what was happening. Hugo looked just as bewildered.

William smiled when he saw them appear onstage. "Here are our performers now, Hugo Baron and Abby Stanton. Let's give them a big welcome."

The audience began to applaud and Abby could see Janet and Margaret seated beside each other in the crowd, both of them grinning up at her.

"Ladies and gentlemen." William's deep voice boomed over the loud speaker. "We are now going to test the skills of our resident ornithologist with the help of the Curator of the Sparrow Island Nature Conservatory, Mr. Hugo Baron."

Another short round of applause followed this announcement.

Giddy anticipation knotted Abby's stomach as she waited to see what they expected of her. Naomi Yardley brought out a wicker basket and handed it to William, who then held it up in the air.

"In this basket," William explained, "are ten cards, each containing the name of a different type of bird." He paused for a moment, scanning the audience. "May I have a volunteer to help us out here?"

"I'll do it!" Bobby shouted, leaping from his chair and running up onto the stage. The audience laughed at his enthusiasm.

"Very good." William waited until Bobby reached him. "Now, son, you just hold this basket until we ask you to draw the first card."

Bobby took the basket from him, smiling from ear to ear.

"Now," William continued, "we'll need to blindfold Dr. Stanton to make certain that this is a true test of her abilities. Hugo, do you have a handkerchief that we can borrow?"

"I do," Hugo replied, pulling a pristine blue silk handkerchief from the breast pocket of his jacket. He folded it into a band, then tied it around Abby's head, covering her eyes.

"Is that too tight?"

"No, it's just fine," she assured him.

Abby stood in the dark, waiting to see what was going to happen next, although she had a fairly good idea.

"I think we're ready," William intoned. "Ladies and gentleman, Bobby will draw a card and show it to all of us. Hugo will then make the appropriate birdcall and it will be up to Abby to make the proper identification. Is everybody ready?"

Abby nodded, eager to begin this unique interactive display of their talents.

She heard the shuffle of paper, then silence descended on the auditorium. A moment later, the sound of a gentle coo filled the air.

"A rock dove," Abby said without hesitation.

The crowd burst into applause, signaling her correct

answer. Eight more birdcalls followed, each one correctly identified by Abby.

"This is it, ladies and gentleman," William said. "The final
birdcall, and it's a tough one. Bobby, the card please."

Abby waited, tension seeping into her veins. She wanted to
get it right so the talent show could end on a high note. Like
Edmonia, she was ready to do it all over again next year.

She craned her head, listening to an odd sort of chirping
rattle. Recognition teased the edges of her brain, but she
couldn't quite place it.

"Would you like to hear it again?" William asked her.

"Yes, please," Abby replied.

Hugo repeated the birdcall for her, making it even louder
than before.

This time she got it. "The belted kingfisher."

The crowd erupted in applause. Abby removed the blindfold and saw them on their feet, giving her and Hugo a standing ovation.

"Good job," Hugo said, moving by her side.

"I couldn't have done it without you. Those birdcalls were
perfect."

He grinned at her. "I guess we make a good team."

Abby had known it all along, even if their friendship had
gone dormant for a short while. Like a perennial flower, it had
blossomed once more, and was basking in the light of trust and
loyalty.

Hugo and Abby bowed to the crowd, then he turned to her
and offered his arm. "Can I still count on you to share a piece
of pie with me?"

She smiled at him, proud to call Hugo her friend. "You can
always count on me."

CHAPTER ❧ TWENTY-TWO

THE FIRST SATURDAY IN May dawned sunny and bright. Abby and Bobby had arisen early to release Quackers and her eight ducklings into the wild. They packed up the mallard family, taking care to preserve the nest as much as possible. That was an integral part to a successful relocation, since the ducklings associated it with their home and mother.

Abby had searched a long time for the perfect spot and finally found it. She carefully moved the nest to a small depression in the ground surrounded by bushes and near a fresh water pond. Tall reeds obfuscated the nest site, making it safer from predators.

Then she and Bobby sat far removed from the mallard family's new home, but still close enough to see and record how the mother duck and the ducklings adapted to their new surroundings.

"Do you think they'll like it here?" Bobby whispered.

"I think they will. There are lots of food sources for them to forage and a pond where the ducklings can learn to swim. I plan to come back often and check on their progress."

"Me too," Bobby said.

Abby had already written extensive journals chronicling the lives of the ducklings from the time the first egg was laid. Though she'd incubated many abandoned eggs in her laboratory, she rarely got a chance to observe a situation like this.

They'd both watched the ducklings hatch in the nest, pulling for them every step of the way as they'd struggled to emerge from their eggs. The natural process was designed to make certain the ducklings were strong enough to make it in the world.

Not all of them were.

Abby knew that was true of humans as well. Both Hugo and Marion Graves had left the nest much too early. One had flourished and the other floundered, but now the men had become friends.

She understood now why Marion had insisted everyone call him by his last name. He'd used that as a wall to push people away after Vanessa's death. If no one got close to him, he couldn't be tempted to take advantage of them again.

Abby smiled to herself, pleased that he'd attended services at Little Flock last week. Marion was slowly emerging from his shell, ready for a new beginning and strong enough this time to do it right.

"What's Quackers doing?" Bobby asked, as the duck chased after an errant duckling, flapping her wings.

"She's keeping them together so they stay safe. The ducklings are still too young to wander far from the nest."

Bobby grinned. "Like the time I wandered over to Mary's

backyard when I was little and started eating some of her violets. I remember my mom scooping me up and carrying me home.

"Just like that," Abby said, happy that the adventurous toddler had chosen to ingest an edible flower.

Bobby looked at his watch. "Hey, we're going to be late for the groundbreaking."

He was right. Abby started to gather up her things, eager to arrive at the library early so she could get a good seat for the groundbreaking ceremony for the new wing.

"Bye, Quackers," Bobby said softly, waving to the mallard.

Abby recognized the bittersweet moment that she'd experienced many times before. She might not have children of her own, but each time she released one of her wildlife patients back into the wild she felt a mixture of both pride and sorrow that made it easier to empathize with parents who suffered through empty-nest syndrome.

Times like this also made her remember one of her favorite Bible verses.

"There is a time for everything, and a season for every activity under heaven: a time to be born and a time to die, a time to plant and a time to uproot" (Ecclesiastes 3:1–2).

"Are you ready?" Bobby asked her, his eyes bright with anticipation.

"Ready," Abby told him. They headed off together to witness the birth of a new season for the Sparrow Island Library.

ABBY SAT IN A CHAIR on the front lawn of the library, waiting for the groundbreaking ceremony to begin.

"Here come the Rileys," Mary said. She was seated beside Abby, her wheelchair fitting perfectly at the end of the front row. They were saving seats for Hugo, their parents and Henry, who all had yet to arrive.

Abby turned to see Paul and Anne talking to Naomi Yardley, though she was surprised to see that Anne's brother, Marion Graves, was nowhere in sight.

"I love Anne's suit," Mary commented as the Rileys walked down the grassy aisle between the rows of white folding chairs. "It's such a pretty color and . . ."

Abby turned to her. "Is something wrong?"

Mary leaned closer and whispered, "Take a look at her left wrist."

Abby glanced at it as the Rileys walked toward the podium. Anne wore a gold and pearl watch that looked exactly like the one that Mary had lost.

"You don't think . . ." Mary murmured, her eyes growing wide.

"No," Abby exclaimed, certain neither of the Rileys could be a thief, "of course not."

"I don't think so either," Mary said in a low voice, "although you have to admit it does seem very odd. Henry told me that my watch was one-of-a-kind when he gave it to me."

Abby knew how much Mary loved that watch. It was all the more special to her because Henry had given it to her. But she could hardly accuse Anne of stealing it.

Before they could discuss it any further, Anne herself approached them.

"Hello, you two," Anne said, adjusting the watch on her wrist. It was a little big and kept sliding down—another sign that it might not belong to her.

Mary exchanged a glance with Abby, then said, "Hello, Anne. This is a big day for the library."

"Isn't it exciting?" Anne said. "Paul and I could hardly sleep last night. So we stayed up late watching some old videos from our photo safari in Africa and now I'm just exhausted." She looked down at her feet. "I'm lucky my shoes match."

"I doubt Marion would let you out of the house if they didn't," Abby teased.

Anne laughed. "You're absolutely right about that, but I haven't seen him today."

"I like your watch," Mary said, folding her hands on her lap. "It looks very much like one I used to own."

"Oh?" Anne held out her arm to admire the watch. "Yes it's very pretty. I wonder where it came from."

Mary arched a brow. "You don't know?"

"Well, we've been so many places," Anne replied. "I just can't be sure. We pick up baubles here and there." A frown line appeared in her forehead as she looked at the watch again. "Although this looks quite expensive. You'd think I would remember it."

"May I look at it?" Mary asked her.

"Of course you may." Anne undid the clasp, then slipped it off her arm and handed it to Mary.

Abby knew from Anne's manner that she was completely unaware that she might be wearing a hot watch on her wrist, which made her wonder how it had gotten there.

She knew what other people might think—that Marion Graves had returned to his life of crime. But she knew Hugo believed he had turned his life around and she did too. Perhaps the watch wasn't one-of-a-kind after all.

Mary looked more closely at the watch, then turned it

over. The expression on her face confirmed that it belonged to her.

"Look at this," Mary said to her sister. Then she held up the watch so that Abby could see the engraving on the back. The inscription read:

For Mary. Love, H.C.

"What is it?" Anne asked, looking between the two of them.

"Anne . . ." Abby began, not certain how to broach the subject. She finally decided to just come out and say it. "The watch you're wearing belongs to my sister. It turned up missing from our deck about a month and a half ago."

A look of horror crossed Anne's face. "Oh no."

"I'm sure you didn't steal it," Mary said. "I'm just so happy to have it back that I don't even care how it got in your possession."

But Mary's words didn't seem to comfort her.

Anne shook her head. "I just can't believe this is happening again. I thought he'd stopped doing that sort of thing . . ."

Disappointment squeezed Abby's chest. If Marion's own beloved sister believed he'd returned to a life of crime, then what was Abby supposed to think?

Paul approached them. "Anne, dear, they're almost ready—" Then he saw the look on his wife's face. "Darling, what's wrong?"

"I was wearing Mary's watch."

"Yes?" he said, clearly not understanding what she was trying to say. "It looks very nice."

"Paul," she began, moving closer to him. "It's happening

again. Mary's watch was stolen from her deck last month. This morning it was on my dresser. You know what this means."

His mouth dropped open. "Oh no!"

"Oh yes," she countered. "After everything we've . . ."

". . . done for him." Paul shook his head. "I thought moving to Sparrow Island would be a . . ."

". . . new beginning for all of us." Anne sighed. "I guess some things . . ."

". . . just never change." Paul turned to Mary. "Please accept our full apologies. We had no idea . . ."

"It's all right," Mary assured him. "Let's just forget it ever happened."

"I'm afraid we can't do that," Paul replied, then he looked past them. "Here comes Marion now."

Abby turned to see Marion Graves walking up the grassy aisle. Unlike his more formal attire when he worked as a butler, today he wore blue denim jeans and a khaki shirt. A dark green backpack was slung over one shoulder.

"Maybe we should wait to talk about this until after the groundbreaking," Abby suggested, glancing helplessly at her sister. This was not the best time or place for a family confrontation.

"There you are," Marion said, finally reaching his sister and brother-in-law. "I was shocked you'd already left the house when I got home from my walk."

"Marion, we have a problem," Anne said solemnly.

"I know." Marion removed the backpack from his shoulder. "Rufus is in trouble again."

Abby could see now that it was partially unzipped and the capuchin monkey's tiny head was peeking out.

"Rufus?" Mary said, looking confused.

Anne nodded. "We thought he'd fully reformed, but it seems that's not the case."

"It's certainly not," Marion replied. "Look at this." Then he unzipped the backpack all the way. After Rufus climbed out, he turned the backpack upside down.

A large collection of jewelry, shiny stones, coins and Abby's miniature magnifying glass tumbled out onto the soft lawn. All items matching the description of items that had gone missing on Sparrow Island the last few weeks.

Marion frowned down at the booty. "It seems Rufus is up to his old tricks again."

Abby stared in disbelief at the monkey. "Are you saying Rufus is the petty thief who's been roaming Sparrow Island?"

"Yes, I'm afraid it's true," Anne replied. "We were so hoping Rufus would . . ."

". . . turn over a new leaf here."

Abby stared at all the stolen loot as the puzzle pieces finally fell into place. "So it was a monkey all along. That explains quite a lot, actually."

Paul picked up the monkey, cradling him in his arms. "The folks at the Sidekick Foundation used to call him . . ."

". . . Sticky Fingers," Anne said with a sigh. "Poor Rufus just can't resist anything shiny. He has to take it for himself and hide it. That's why he flunked out. He kept stealing things wherever he went."

Abby bit back a smile. "Sticky Fingers?"

"Yes," Anne said, her mouth twitching with amusement. "The poor little guy just can't seem to help himself. Although we had no—"

"—idea that he'd discovered a way to get out of the house."

Paul looked at his brother-in-law. "Where did you find all of this?"

Marion folded his arms across his chest. "I found both Rufus and his stash near the conservatory while I was out on my morning walk. Who knows how long he's been going back and forth between there and the house."

A light went off in Abby's head. "I think I may have something that belongs to one of you." She reached for her purse and pulled out the two Burmese coins that had been found in her lab. "Do these look familiar?"

Marion reached out to take them, his face contorting. "They're mine. Vanessa sent them to me while I was in jail, shortly before she died."

Paul placed a comforting hand on his back as Marion struggled to gather himself.

"She wrote to me that our love was like these two coins," Marion continued. "Rare, precious and able to withstand the sands of time. Thank you for bringing them back to me."

Anne looked up at Abby. "Wherever did you find them?"

"Bobby McDonald found one of them in an empty cage in my laboratory," Abby explained. "I found the other in a bucket in the same building, but that was several days later and that bucket hadn't been there when we found the first one."

"Rufus must have gotten in the building somehow," Mary ventured. "More than once from the sound of it."

Abby shook her head. "I don't see how. That door's usually locked both day and night."

"Are the windows locked, too?" Marion asked her.

That possibility hadn't occurred to her. "No, they're too high for an intruder to climb." Then she looked at Rufus, who looked back at her with his sweet and innocent expression. "Unless he's a monkey."

"Rufus learned to open windows as part of his training at the Sidekick Foundation," Marion informed her. "He's probably been inside every building on the conservatory grounds."

That explained how Quackers had gotten out of his cage. Rufus had probably opened the cage door, then run off to cause some more mischief.

Then another thought occurred to Abby. "Is it possible that Rufus is the one who tore apart the Rites of Spring exhibit?"

"Very possible, I'm afraid," Marion replied. "He'd think it was a playground."

"Oh, Abby," Paul said with a groan. "I'm so sorry . . ."

"I'm not," she told him, forestalling his apology. "I'd much rather have Rufus be the reason behind it than some unidentified vandal. I had wondered why nothing was destroyed, just tossed about and all in a jumble."

"He stole Mary's watch too," Anne told her brother. "I've never been so mortified in my life. Or worn stolen property before!"

Mary laughed. "You didn't know it was stolen. Besides, I'm just happy to have my watch back. I think this is going to turn out to be a great day."

Abby agreed. It was so nice to have everything on Sparrow Island back to normal. No malicious petty thief or vandal roamed the island. Just good people and a variety of wildlife, all doing their best to live together in harmony.

As the chairs set out for the groundbreaking ceremony began to fill up, Naomi Yardley took the podium. "I think it's time for us to get started."

Everyone returned to their seats, Hugo, Henry and Abby's parents arriving just in time. Abby saw Marion seated beside Hugo with Rufus sitting docilely in his lap. The monkey was staring in fascination at the brass buttons on Hugo's jacket.

"We will begin this morning's ceremony with a short passage from the latest publication in children's literature by Paul and Anne Riley," Naomi announced. Then she turned to the guests of honor. "Paul, could you please do the honor of reading it for us?"

Abby listened as Paul read the opening pages of their latest book, a child's adventure tale set on Sparrow Island. She'd gotten a sneak preview of it a week ago and couldn't wait to buy a copy of her own.

The last line of the book was her favorite and one she would always remember.

On Sparrow Island, good friends are never far away.

A NOTE FROM THE EDITORS

THIS ORIGINAL BOOK WAS created by the Books and Inspirational Media Division of Guideposts, the world's leading inspirational publisher. Founded in 1945 by Dr. Norman Vincent Peale and his wife Ruth Stafford Peale, Guideposts helps people from all walks of life achieve their maximum personal and spiritual potential. Guideposts is committed to communicating positive, faith-filled principles for people everywhere to use in successful daily living.

Our publications include award-winning magazines like *Guideposts, Angels on Earth, Sweet 16* and *Positive Thinking,* best-selling books, and outreach services that demonstrate what can happen when faith and positive thinking are applied to day-to-day life.

For more information, visit us online at www.guideposts.org, call (800) 431-2344 or write Guideposts, 39 Seminary Hill Road, Carmel, New York 10512.